Listen,
Do You Want
to Know a
Secret

Listen, Do You Want to Know a Secret

A Swinging Sixties Mystery

Teresa Trent

LEVEL
BEST BOOKS

Historia
ESTABLISHED 1959

Author Photo Credit: M.K. Higginbotham

First edition

ISBN: 978-1-68512-549-3

Cover art by Level Best Designs

This book was professionally typeset on Reedsy.
Find out more at reedsy.com

In memory of Dawn Dowdle, my agent. She saw something in me I didn't see in myself and for that I will always be thankful.

Praise for the Swinging Sixties Mysteries:

"In Teresa Trent's second book for the Swinging Singles Series, she once again offers a unique story with an engaging cast of characters. Dot Morgan, devastated after witnessing a presidential assassination, steps into a new job, and loses a trusted ally while remaining innocent and flexing to understand the opportunities 1963 offers women. A must-read for any reader who enjoys stepping back into the 'swinging sixties.'"—Terry Korth Fischer, author of the Rory Naysmith Mystery Series

"In author Teresa Trent's *If I Had a Hammer*, President John F. Kennedy's shocking 1963 assassination triggers a sea change in a young eye-witness. Returning to a small-town secretarial job, the heroine becomes entangled in local murder investigations. While trying to solve the crimes, she realizes new possibilities and potential. This mystery's a nostalgic treat for babyboomers."—Linda Lovely, author of the HOA Mysteries

"Mix great music, bellbottoms, and counterculture in with one of the most turbulent times in American history for a groovy setting full of peace, love, and of course, a murder that turns secretary, Dot Morgan's life upside down. She has to solve the mystery before someone else ends up dead. Trent's latest, *If I Had a Hammer*, the second in her Swinging Sixties Mysteries, is a twisty mystery and a fun trip back to a generation that changed everything."—Heather Weidner, author of the Jules Keene Glamping Mysteries and the Mermaid Bay Christmas Shoppe Mysteries

Chapter One

February 9, 1964

"Hurry, Ellie. It's about to start," Al called out.

"I'm just putting the popcorn in the bowl, Al. Keep your shirt on," Ellie yelled back. The jaunty theme song to *My Favorite Martian* played in the background as it capped off the adventures of everyone's favorite Uncle Martin.

"You're not even married yet," Ben said, "and you already sound like an old married couple."

"Yeah, well," Al said as Ellie squeezed in next to him, reaching for a handful of popcorn. "I don't have to report to prison until June." He gave us a smile, cheeks bulging with popcorn. "Isn't that right, sweetie?" He looked like a mischievous squirrel.

Ellie gave him a sour grin and then playfully hit his shoulder. "You're the luckiest man in the world." She lowered her nose slightly, giving Al a piercing, no-nonsense gaze. "Go on and admit it."

"Yes, dear," Al responded automatically. I loved the way they bantered back and forth. You could tell they loved each other dearly.

Ben reached out and took my hand on the crowded couch, and I laid my head on his shoulder. What we had was different, but that was because we hadn't been dating as long as Al and Ellie had. I tried to keep that in mind. Meanwhile, Ed Sullivan appeared in front of the gray-toned curtains. When they panned the audience, it was filled with women. Young women and they all looked like they were about to witness the second coming. There were so many expectant looks to the stage. One girl had her fists clenched and held to her chin. I had seen The Ed Sullivan Show for years, but never had I witnessed such awe-filled excitement.

"Just look at them all." Ellie squinted at the television. "Do you see any men?"

Instead of answering her question, Al added, "Do you see anyone over thirty?"

Ed Sullivan looked somewhere between excited and terrified. "Ladies and gentlemen, the Beatles," Ed Sullivan yelled, and the screams rose to a feverish pitch.

I had never witnessed mass hysteria but was sure I was seeing it on Ellie's new Phillips television set. "This is unbelievable. Those girls are going insane." The camera went from the audience to John, Paul, and George. Ringo was set up on a raised platform with his drums. They knocked out "I Want to Hold Your Hand," and with each measure, the crowd screamed even more.

"I can barely hear the song for the caterwauling going on in the background," Al said.

"I wonder if they can hear each other." Ellie popped a handful of popcorn into her mouth.

"I told you the Beatles were big news." Ben was the room's professional reporter.

I couldn't get over how excited the fans were. I considered myself a bit of an expert in popular music since I landed my job at KDUD, *The Smile on Your Dial*. I wasn't spinning records, but I was answering the request line. We were getting more and more requests for the Beatles. Unfortunately, my boss chose Perry Como over John Lennon and Montavoni over Paul McCartney. Sometimes it felt like I was spending my days in a department store, listening to never-ending soulless melodies. Sales were down, and our listenership was too. If my boss would only switch to the popular music of the day, we'd be playing in everyone's kitchen.

It was more than these girls' crazy behavior in the presence of the Beatles.

They bought the records. This was a big industry, and these four kids from England were taking America by storm. The rival station across town, KOOL, was playing them nonstop, and that's who people were listening to on their radios. Ellie told me they even made jokes about our station. We were oldies for the oldies. As Charlie Brown would say, "Good grief."

I needed to count my blessings. I had a job I enjoyed. I just hated to see how they were missing an opportunity with their choice of music.

"Oh, my." Ellie had her hand on her heart. "I've never seen anything like it."

Al nudged her. "Don't tell me you're having heart palpitations. Isn't that what brides-to-be do in all those old movies?"

Ellie shot Al a look. "Don't be silly. Watching these four men, I feel like we're on the precipice of a new movement. All those soapy songs from the fifties are being replaced by music you can actually dance to." She grabbed Al's hand and pulled him off the couch, popcorn flying. "Come on, dance with me."

Al obliged her and pushed back the coffee table. They danced next to the couch.

I waited for Ben to do the same, but he had chosen that moment to dive into the remaining popcorn. Here we were, five days from Valentine's Day and, well...

I grabbed his hand, causing more popcorn to fly. "Let's dance."

He pointed to the TV. "But I was watching that."

"You'd better go along there, brother. It's easier than arguing," Al lamented happily.

Chapter Two

May 1964

I hummed along with the music at KDUD Radio, *Your Smile on Your Dial.* I had settled in well and I liked the people here. They were nice, especially compared to my last position at Gibson Construction. I had been on the job for less than a month when I was fired. It was a big ugly stain on my resume, but with my boyfriend Ben Dalton's help, I got a job at KDUD. I answer the phone and listen to music all day, which is great, even if it's Frank Sinatra singing "Three Coins in the Fountain." My boss, Holden Ramsey, loves that one. He isn't too bad to work for. His temperament is easier to live with than my last boss. Not only that, but we have a station cat named Uncle George. He is as mellow as the music around here, with a constant purr if he's being petted. A cat makes a workplace feel more like a home.

When I first get here in the morning, if we have someone important coming to the radio station, Holden likes for me to straighten up the lobby. First impressions are the most important, he always says. That's what I was doing when I came upon a piece of sheet music for the song "Love Will Find a Way." It was wedged under the couch, so I got on my hands and knees and tried to pull it out, causing my behind to rise in the air.

"My, my," a male voice said from behind me. "What are you doing down there?" Gerald Watson, the DJ who ran the station during the night, had walked in, and I hadn't heard him. When I scrambled up, he was rubbing the back of his neck. He was the first colored person I had ever worked with, but it didn't seem to matter to either of us. Here I was, a girl in my twenties who was constantly compared to Sandra Dee, while Gerald looked more like Sidney Poitier in one of his brainier roles.

Gerald let out a yawn.

"You look tired today, Gerald. Rough night?"

He grinned from the corner of his mouth, answering sarcastically. "How can I complain about my dream job? At least I don't have to listen to all the oldies you get on your shift."

Gerald's show, *Jammin' with Gerry*, was much more entertaining than Holden's fare. He mostly played hits by black artists, which probably ruffled some of the town's feathers, but the music was wonderful. Mary Wells, Ray Charles, Aretha Franklin. Add to that Gerald's low velvety voice between the recordings and you didn't want to turn away. He answered his own request line, and you can bet he was getting more calls than Holden was during the day.

Gerald groaned. "What he doesn't understand is the audience at night wants different music. We can only take so much Perry Como in this world."

When he wasn't playing Frank Sinatra, Holden played Como, his favorite being "Catch a Falling Star." I had to push him to get him to play some of the Beatles' hits. It was only May, and they already had two hits on the chart. Still, we were forced to listen to the ballads of Perry Como and Dean Martin the entire day.

I held up the paper sticking out from under the couch in the front lobby. "Do you have any idea where this came from?"

Before he could answer, the phone rang. I hoped it was a request or something that would keep me busy. It had been a slow start to the day. "Yeah." The voice on the other end had a thick country accent. "Don't you got anything more than Montavoni? I like KOOL. That's the station that plays the hits. Not KDUD." Instead of making our station call letters sound like "dude," the caller emphasized "dud."

The caller laughed on the phone and hung up.

"Another one!" I slammed down the phone. "Those guys over at KOOL can't stop pranking me. I know that was the DJ, and he loves to make a fool out of me and put these calls on the air. It's harassment."

"Yeah, well, there's no law against idiots harassing people," Gerald said, with something untold in his eyes.

I picked up the sheet music again. "Okay. Where were we? Do you know where this music came from?"

Gerald took the paper from me and, not meeting my eyes, commented, "I...I don't have any idea why it's here."

There was something shifty about the way he was acting. Could this be his sheet music? Did Gerald aspire to be a singer? If so, why not just tell me? He wouldn't be the first DJ to use announcing music as a stepping stone to singing it. "Strange to find it. It's not as if we have live music going on here."

Gerald swallowed and looked up with earnest brown eyes. His lashes were beautiful, and as a blond, I wished mine stood out like that. "But we could. That old recording studio is still in the back, and Holden has done nothing with it. He was so worried about the radio station making money. He needs to understand that with a few good sound engineers, he could make a pretty little profit from that little recording studio the Schultz family left in the back."

This surprised me. I had seen the studio, but it was ridiculously small. The former owner used it for gospel broadcasts. "Really? People really record things around here? I mean, Camden, Texas, is not a very big town."

"It's not the size of the town, but the access to a recording studio. Everybody wants to get their voice on a record. You just have to have a good sound engineer and a band worth recording."

The idea of making a record was as foreign to me as meeting a president. That was something other people did. "Do you know any sound engineers?"

Gerald shrugged. "I know how to run a board. It's not that hard." In my months of working at KDUD, this was a side of him I hadn't seen. He was confident and self-assured.

"Have you told Holden this?"

"Yeah." He let out a soft chuckle. "I'm not sure whether it's because Holden is afraid of anything that has to do with modern electronics, or that the person who asked him doesn't share the same skin color."

"Really?"

"You're young, Dot. But not everybody is kind to people who look like me around here. You should know that, but you don't understand how life is. You act like we're the same, which is unusual in this town."

"I thought we were, sort of."

Gerald smiled, "And that's what I love about you, Miss Dot. Your story should be titled, *Gidget Goes into Radio*."

Before I could say anything else, a thin woman with a nose too large for her face slammed through the door to stand in front of me, her hair pulled back in a severe ponytail. Tortoiseshell glasses revealed a determined look in her eyes. She clutched a newspaper to her chest.

She pushed past me.

"Can I help you?" I asked, hoping she wasn't going to yell at me for something she heard on the radio and disliked.

"I need to see Holden. Right now."

I returned to my desk and took out a pad of paper. "Mr. Ramsey is on the air at the moment, ma'am. I'll be glad to take your name and number and have him call you."

She clutched the newspaper even tighter. She looked over at Gerald, held his gaze, and then, dismissing him, came back. "No. I do not want to leave my name and number. I need to speak to him now, and if you don't let me in there, then I'll go in and announce it on the radio. You want that to happen?" From the looks of her flushed face and resolute expression, I didn't want to take her up on her dare.

"No, ma'am. Just give me a minute. What's your name?"

"Joyce Bishop."

I walked into the soundproof DJ booth as Holden was introducing Perry Como's latest reworked version of "Love Makes the World Go Round." He looked up, a little annoyed, and then held up a hand as he spoke into the microphone. He took on the persona of a dreamy-eyed announcer with a pleasant smile on his face. "Let's drift off this morning to this beautiful tune on KDUD."

7

He turned off the mic and scowled, his voice instantly changing. Holden was a handsome man, but with this quick turn of expression, he looked older than I had originally thought. "What do you want? I told you never to come in here when I'm working."

"I realize that, but you have a visitor who is insisting on seeing you."

He replaced a record in a paper sleeve and, not looking up from his work, asked, "Who is it?"

"She says her name is Joyce Bishop, and she's not too happy."

Holden filed the record with such a snap that I was afraid he had broken it. He then glanced out into the lobby, his gaze lighting on his guest. "Tell Gerald to come in here to cover for me."

Exiting the booth, I grabbed Gerald. "Would you sit in for Holden for a few minutes?"

"Sure." Gerald switched places with Holden, who then warily walked to his visitor.

Joyce held up a newspaper. "I can't believe it. You're engaged to yet another woman?"

"Hello, Joyce." Compared to her, his voice was calm, or at least he was trying to make it sound that way. He pitched his head slightly and crossed his arms in front of him.

"You are a murderer," she said, accenting every syllable with jarring head moves that reminded me of a chicken pecking for corn.

It was at this moment I was thinking I needed a break. I didn't want to further embarrass my boss by sticking around to hear this woman's wild accusations.

"I'll just leave you two to talk." I started backing away, but Holden gestured for me to stay.

He smirked. "So, go to the police. Aren't they the ones you should see about this?"

Joyce pulled one hand off the paper and then pointed at him with her index finger. "You know what I mean. You killed that other woman you were married to, and I've had a few nights when I wondered if you would kill me. I've heard you creeping around in the bushes. I know it was you. Just because

I can't prove it, doesn't mean it didn't happen. Who is it you're marrying this time?" She pulled the paper in front of her glasses. "Some woman named Magnolia Daniels. Where do you get a name like that?"

He gave a haughty lift to his chin. "Magnolia Daniels is part of *the* Daniels family. She is not some wrong-side-of-the-tracks woman like you are."

Holden seemed like a nice, easy-going guy in the station, but DJs, like actors, are sometimes nothing like the person they present to the public. I surmised this Joyce woman must be a real thorn in his side, especially if she was going around accusing him of murder. Holden, with those big blue eyes, couldn't murder anyone. Yes, I had just seen his quick temper when I interrupted him, but I warmed up to him again as if he hadn't just name-dropped a town society name. The angry, bespectacled woman was obviously not well.

Holden turned. "That's all I have to say on the matter." He motioned to me like I was a bouncer, ready to wrestle someone out of the station. "If you would see Miss Bishop out?"

All I could do was answer, "Yes, sir."

Holden went to the next room while I was stuck facing Joyce Bishop, who had at least an inch on me. Her gaze, however, was still on my boss.

"I'm so sorry. I need to ask you to leave."

Finally, she looked at me. "Fine. But this isn't over yet. I'm going to make sure of it. I wonder if the *Camden Courier* would be interested in this story."

Once Joyce left the station, I found Holden down the hall in the sales office, running a hand through his slicked-back salt-and-pepper hair. He looked at me, and the familiar, easy-to-work-with manner he'd had returned. "Well, that was crazy, wasn't it?"

I was about to answer when Holden's fiancée, Magnolia Daniels, yoo-hooed from the lobby.

Holden straightened himself out and returned to the lobby with me following, feeling guilty for not being at my desk.

Magnolia stood in the doorway wearing a white cotton dress and an enormous sun hat with a wide yellow band. Magnolia's outfits were straight out of the style magazines, where mine drifted more to the sales at JC Penney. "Who was that woman in the parking lot? She nearly hit me with her car."

As she took off the hat, her chestnut brown hair fell in waves around her shoulders.

"She's nobody, darling." Holden kissed Magnolia on the cheek. "What brings you here this morning? I thought you were going to Dallas to look for a wedding dress." Holden's entire attitude had flipped from the caustic words he shared with Joyce to syrupy sweet with Magnolia.

"Oh, I was, but I changed my mind. You know I want Ellie Monroe to make it over at Bluebonnets, but she's so busy this time of year. She told me I had to decide by a certain date, but I needed more time to shop and compare. I am the bride, after all."

Besides being in wedding season, my cousin Ellie was consumed right now with details for her own wedding. Her upcoming trip to the altar had seen a lot of turbulence, and the sooner we got back to normal life, the better. She fit me for my maid of honor dress for her wedding way back in March. It was a lovely light blue dress that fit today's style above the knee. Ellie's head was spinning with flowers and photographers, cakes, and place cards. The one thing she kept putting off was her own wedding dress. As usual, she put herself last. I was worried she'd have a nervous breakdown before she ever met Al at the front of the church.

I hesitated, then spoke. "Ellie's my cousin. Wedding season is crazy for her."

Magnolia's kohl-lined eyes brightened. "She's your cousin? That's wonderful! I had no idea. Could you please," she put her hands in prayer position," please, please talk to your cousin and tell her I won't be happy unless she makes my dress? I've looked at all the dresses in Dallas, and the one she sketched up for me is exactly what I want. I should have agreed to do it, but checked Dallas first. Now it's too late. Could you talk to her? Please?"

Ellie was slammed with work, but Magnolia looked desperate. It was good business for Ellie to make a dress for the noted Daniels family. "I can talk to her, but no guarantees."

Magnolia laughed. "Just what your cousin said."

"She's also getting married this summer, so she has a lot of things keeping her busy. The thing is, she tries to do everything herself. Why don't you try to convince her to hire another seamstress until her wedding is over?"

Magnolia cocked her head to the side and then pulled out a pair of sunglasses and put them on, making her look like Audrey Hepburn from *Breakfast at Tiffany's*. "I could do that. Most definitely, but only if you come with me. She might listen to you."

"That's a great idea," Holden said. "I could call my mother to go with you, if you'd like?"

Magnolia smiled at his idea. She was a striking woman and had all the beauty money could buy. "That would be great."

I looked at Holden, who nodded his permission. "Sure."

Magnolia kissed Holden on the cheek. "Ciao, darling. Thanks to Dot here, I might convince Cousin Ellie to make the most beautiful dress in the world. You won't be able to control yourself when you see me walk down that aisle."

He took her hand and kissed it. "I can't control myself now." His eyes were warm as he pulled her closer.

She let out a soft giggle. I was feeling a tad bit uncomfortable, but then Magnolia pulled away and headed out the door, the scent of expensive perfume trailing behind her.

After Magnolia left, Gerald came in from the DJ booth.

"Okay, boss. I have a long commercial on right now, so that should get you ample time to get back in the booth."

"Thanks, man. I really appreciate you stepping in like that."

Gerald gave a little smile and then raised a hand to his chin. "Sounds like you've got trouble. What was going on with that crazy woman?"

I wanted to hear the answer to that, too. "You missed the best part, but she said that our boss had something to do with the death of a woman he was previously engaged to." I met Holden's gaze. "Is that right?"

Holden shoved his hands into the pockets of his well-creased khaki pants. With Holden, nothing was ever wrinkled, and even if a hair fell out of place, he looked like an ad out of Sears and Roebuck in the "Man About Town" section. "This is just what I'm talking about. Joyce Bishop is crazy. She and I dated a few years ago, but it didn't take me long to figure out she was not all there. She's nothing more than a paranoid spinster. She was always accusing me of things that I didn't do. Joyce is a weird girl from a strange family."

"So, who was the woman she was talking about?"

Holden gulped, but then Gerald backed me up. "So, there is actually some woman out there that she thinks you caused harm to?"

Holden's eyes widened. He was trying to control his emotions. "No. I do not know what she's talking about."

Gerald gave Holden a sideways glance. "People just don't go around saying things like that unless there's a drop of truth to them. It sure wouldn't look good if she mouthed off to somebody else."

Holden came closer to both of us as if we were in a football huddle. "Exactly. She is out to do me some sort of personal damage, probably because she saw our engagement picture in the paper. Just look how close she was to telling Magnolia all of this crazy stuff." Holden continued. "I need to ask you both a favor. Call it professional or personal, I don't care. I'm trying to make a go of this radio station. False charges could be disastrous for KDUD and your jobs."

If anybody asked me, I would say it had to do with the soupy music he played, but no one had.

Holden kept talking. "So, please keep what happened here this morning to yourselves."

I couldn't imagine who I would want to tell something like that, but nodded to reassure Holden.

"Sure, boss," Gerald said.

"If Magnolia were to have found out, it could be the end of our engagement. I don't know if you've noticed this or not, but I'm in love with that woman, and I would do anything, anything at all, to make this marriage go forward."

I knew that was the truth. Whenever Magnolia came into the room, all his attention turned to her. It didn't hurt there was a twenty-year age difference between the two, and she looked like someone from *Vanity Fair*, but she seemed equally enamored with him, and that was all that mattered. I could understand his reasons for keeping this woman's accusations quiet. True love doesn't come along every day. The commercial jingle for smooth-tasting cigarettes was about to go off the air, and Holden looked up at the clock.

"I've got to get back to the booth now, but thank you so much for helping me to manage the situation." With that, he returned to the glassed-in room next door and put the headphones on.

Gerald and I stood there for a moment until, finally, he said, "I don't know about this, Dot. If what he says is true, then that's okay, but what if there was some sort of truth to what she was saying? Neither of us was around during that time."

Was there a grain of truth in what Joyce Bishop said, and were we putting Magnolia Daniels in danger by agreeing to keep it from her? I wasn't sure if I was doing the right thing or not. I had only been working at KDUD for a few months, so I didn't know that much about Holden Ramsey's background. Was he an abuser with a long history of victims? Was I aiding someone who battered women? I looked up at Holden through the glass. "I don't feel good about this either. I guess for now, we just wait and see."

"And if it's true?"

"Then we talk."

Chapter Three

The next day, I joined Magnolia and Holden's mother, Leah Ramsey at the Bluebonnets Dress Shop for a fitting and general discussion of Magnolia's dress. Ellie agreed to add Magnolia to her busy schedule after Holden's mother put some pressure on. I thought I was the one who was supposed to do that. Holden's mother had a way of making herself the decision-maker on any occasion. When Leah and Magnolia weren't looking, I mouthed a "Sorry" in her direction. Ellie was pleased to have me there because she'd been ganged up on by troublesome brides and their mothers many times. It was good to have someone on her side.

Bluebonnets Dress Shop could have been renamed Bluebonnets Bridal Shop this morning as several brides walked back and forth, looking at off-the-rack dresses. Ellie made wedding dresses, but she also bought from a clothing distributor to always have plenty of stock on hand. Mothers and daughters haunted Bluebonnets, and it was the best place to get a wedding dress in North Texas. I recognized one girl from my graduating class going through the rack of dresses rapid-fire clicking the hangers against the metal dress rack. This was serious business. It was tough trying to find the exact right combination of froth and femininity for this special occasion.

Magnolia stood on a raised staging area, looking at herself in three floor-to-ceiling mirrors. According to Ellie, they were down to two options.

"You can go very modern in a shorter style and make your wedding look very dramatic, or you can go with a more traditional style with a classic gown complete with pearl buttons down the back. The choice is yours, but I have to tell you if you go with the more classic style dress, it takes time to put something like that together. Just when is your wedding again?" Ellie stood with a clipboard in hand, ready to record the vital information.

"I'm afraid I've been wasting time looking at dresses in Dallas. It's in August. That ought to give you enough time, right?"

Ellie raised her eyebrows. "August?" She tried to remain professional, but I knew she was calculating how long it would take to make the dress and go on a honeymoon with Al.

Ellie took a breath.

Magnolia gazed at herself in the mirror. "I really like this style, but can you see how it's a little loose at the waist? She fingered the fabric rose on the neckline. "And these would have to go. I think they block the sleek line of the bodice. You see why I need to have one made? I have very specific tastes, which is why you just have to design me a dress exactly to my vision."

Leah stepped forward and placed a bridal veil on Magnolia's head. "Oh my. You will be a beautiful bride. I think Miss Ellie here will make you a fabulous dress and, of course, it will be on time. I know of at least three girls who had their dresses made here, and they were all quite pleased with them. Ellie makes the finest wedding dresses in the entire county. I just wish your own mother were here with us today to see her daughter."

Magnolia adjusted the veil on her head, staring into the mirror. "I'm glad you're here. That's all that matters."

Where was her mother? If I was getting married, I couldn't keep my mother out of something like this. This was a special day for Magnolia, but just as special for her mother.

"My pleasure," Leah said, giving her future daughter-in-law a brief hug around the shoulders. Then she took her hands and delicately spread out the veil to its full width over Magnolia's shoulders. I wasn't sure who was more excited, the bride-to-be or the mother-in-law.

Magnolia looked over at me. "What do you think?"

"The veil?" I stepped forward. "Leah is right. Everything looks wonderful on you."

"What kind of wedding gown do you think I should wear? Should it be modern or traditional?"

Before I could comment, Leah cut in. "Oh, my dear, I know you didn't ask me, but I think with your family's background, they would want to see you in a traditional dress. Remember, your wedding will be on the society page. You're a classic beauty, and something that's modern and short is just going to look like some sort of tea dress. No, I think you need to go all the way with the traditional wedding dress and veil."

"You do?" Magnolia turned back. "What do you think, Dot?"

I shuddered slightly, trying to give her the answer she wanted, but it was a loaded question. "I think it's up to you. I know you want to please everyone, but think about what will be most comfortable that day. Did you ever plan your wedding when you were a little girl?"

Ellie jumped at that. I had heard her say that phrase many times to get brides to be decisive. "Yes. We all did it, right?"

Magnolia fingered the lace of the veil, her eyes moving upward to the ceiling in thought. "I guess I did."

"And what were you wearing?" Ellie asked, her pen poised.

"I was wearing a traditional wedding dress."

"Perfect!" Leah said, clapping her hands and jumping up slightly.

"But it was pink," Magnolia added.

"Pink?" Leah's smile dropped like a wedding ring off a squirrely ring bearer's pillow.

Magnolia shrugged. "Well, you asked what I thought about when I was a little girl. The dress was pink."

"No bride wears pink down the aisle. You must wear white because it shows purity," Leah whispered in a lowered voice.

"Is that why they wear white?" Magnolia asked.

Leah turned to Ellie. "Tell her about it, Ellie. All brides should look virginal on their wedding days. It symbolizes purity. I'm sure you're wearing white, aren't you?"

Ellie blushed and smiled. "That's what they used to say. Now, it's just a tradition. It's not like the past. Now some girls wear miniskirts and boots. It's wild."

Magnolia seemed pleased with that. "See? Pink is okay."

Ellie smiled. "I could put a touch of pink here and there, but I wouldn't go for the whole dress. Take a day to consider which look you want and then call me tomorrow, but don't let it go much longer because my schedule is filling up."

Magnolia nodded, then looked at me. "Dot said because you have your own wedding coming up, you may hire another seamstress. Do you think that's possible?"

Ellie shot me a look as her lips thinned. "Don't you worry about that, Magnolia. Whatever you decide, we'll handle it."

"Excellent," Leah squealed. "Now, what do you say that you get out of that dress and we go to lunch, Magnolia?"

Ellie quickly removed the bridal veil, and we helped Magnolia step down from the platform in the voluminous dress. Even though I had been asked to come to the appointment, lunch didn't seem included for me. Once they left, Ellie looked at the other two shopping brides and then pulled me behind the counter. "Really? You told her I was going to hire somebody?"

"I told her you *might* hire somebody. Admit it. You're overwhelmed with everything going on right now. There is no way you can have a busy wedding season without a little help."

Ellie picked up a roll of lace and put it up on a rack with great efficiency. "I can handle it."

"Yes, you can, but that doesn't mean you have to. For once in your life, accept you don't have to do everything. Hire someone." My cousin was the most stubborn person I knew.

"And just who do you suggest I hire?" She snapped.

"Every girl in Camden had to take home economics. Everyone knows how to sew, and I'm sure there are some women out there who are looking for a way to make some extra money. Just think about it."

The phone on the counter rang, and Ellie quickly answered it. She was glad to be out of our conversation, and it showed in her quick and curt answer. "Bluebonnets Dress Shop." Her tough stance changed instantly, and she smiled, curling the phone cord around her finger lazily. "That sounds like a wonderful idea, Al, but I'm afraid today I'm just too busy to go to lunch."

There was a pause as Al spoke on the other side. Finally, Ellie spoke, still smiling. "I love you too, and I can't wait to marry you, but I can't go to lunch today. Love you, love you." She hung up the phone and then picked up the clipboard, pulling the notes on Magnolia and then placing them in a file folder. "How do I get Al to understand wedding season for me is like a tax accountant in April?"

"He knows that by now. I think he's just thrilled that you two are getting married and wants to see you. There's no crime in that."

Ellie brought her lips up into a gentle smile. She then put a hand on my shoulder. "Yeah, me and my happily off-white dress. Sorry I fussed at you. I'll think about hiring another person."

"You won't regret it."

"That's what you keep telling me. Listen, could you do me a favor?"

I looked at my watch. "I should get back to work."

"I thought riding along with the bride-to-be was your job this morning. On your way back to the radio station, I need you to stop by your parents' house. Your mom promised we could use her serving platter with the doves on it. Could you pick that up for me? My mom put it on my duty roster, as she likes to call it, but you can see how busy I am here."

Aunt Mavis had taken on her role as mother-of-the-bride like a commanding officer going into battle. It was the least I could do.

Chapter Four

I stopped over at my parents' house, hoping Holden wouldn't put together the meeting at the dress shop was finished. I made a promise to myself that I wouldn't take long because being late was noted in my last job. I guess I always have stuff going on. My mother usually worked at the library Monday through Friday, but she had today off after filling in for a coworker on a busy Saturday. As I walked into the house, Hank Williams was singing about a cheating heart on the stereo.

"Mom?" Normally, I would find her curled up on the couch with a book or working in the kitchen. After checking both locations, I called her again. "Mom?"

My mother came out of my old bedroom after just a minute. She looked a little surprised to see me, and she was out of breath, as if she had rushed to hide what she was doing.

"What's going on?"

My mother ran her hand through her chin-length brown hair. She had a slight overbite and an angular nose, looking like a casting call city librarian. Today, she wore her familiar blue cardigan, plaid skirt, and white blouse. She gave me a nervous giggle. "Oh, nothing. Nothing at all. What brings you by?"

The faster she talked, the more I knew she was up to something. I walked past her and followed her path to my old room. I worried she had changed the paint or wallpaper, and even though I was out of the house, I wasn't ready to lose my childhood room. A Smith Corona typewriter sat against the wall with a piece of paper stuck out of the top. I looked over and read the words on the paper.

Felicia walked into the barn, and there she saw the handsome soldier's shoulders of Jacob as he hefted the hay into the hayloft. He turned to look at her, love smoldering deep in his eyes. She caught her breath as her bosom heaved upward. He was her everything.

"What is this?" I pointed to the words typed in the typewriter.

My mother's face turned a deep red, and she placed her fingers on her neck nervously.

"Nothing." She quickly pulled the paper out of the typewriter and put it on a neat pile set next to it. Every sheet of paper was filled with words.

"Are you writing a book?"

She fluttered her hands, looking like a child caught coloring on the walls. "Oh, I call it that. I'm just playing around. You know, I see so many books in the library and always wondered what it would be like to write one."

"Is it a romance? Like one of those Harlequins Ellie reads?" Some of those books got heated. This was not something I wanted to think of as being written by my mother. Mothers were for home-cooked meals and kisses on boo-boos, not heaving breasts and wily handsome men.

She blushed further. "I know it sounds silly, but I figured a romance would be the easiest thing to write. I'm still not sure if I'm that romantic."

"From what I read, it looked pretty steamy to me."

A little smile played on the corners of my mother's mouth. She looked pleasantly surprised. "Did it?"

"Oh yes." Her writing exercise made me think of her and my father, and then I wished I hadn't.

Then, the look on my mother's face changed. She pressed her lips together and folded her thin arms across her cardigan. "Do you think it's silly?"

I thought it was a little silly, but she looked so vulnerable, I decided I would keep it to myself. "Does it make you happy?"

She stopped for a moment, looking surprised at my question, and then nodded her head. "Yes. It does. I don't really know what I'm doing, but it's just kind of fun."

"Then do it."

She beamed, and her expression was priceless. She really was having fun, and why not? She was my mother, and she could do anything she set her mind to.

"I never thought of myself as a writer, you know, like Ben, your—" her smile widened. "—boyfriend. Can we call him your boyfriend yet?"

"Maybe. We're still in that in-between phase."

"Well, he writes for the newspaper, but this is so much different."

"Do you want me to ask him to read some of your stuff?"

My mother gasped. "Oh no. I'm embarrassed, having you read this, let alone him. He's a man."

"You do realize the rest of the world would read it if you had it published."

She looked as if that thought had just occurred to her. "I guess so," she whispered. "This is silly." She grabbed the stack of typed paper and tucked it into the desk drawer, out of sight. If I had written such salacious material, I think I'd hide it, too. Smoothing her skirt of invisible wrinkles, she asked, "Why did you stop over today?"

"Oh, Ellie asked me to pick up the serving platter. She wants to get everything in place early for the wedding."

"I'll get it for you." My mother stepped by me to go to the kitchen, and I followed. "How is she doing on making her wedding dress?"

"Not good. Seems she's put it at the bottom of her to do list."

She opened an upper cabinet and took out a large serving platter. We usually used it for turkey at Thanksgiving and for big slices of ham at Easter. She handed it to me. "Here you go."

"Thanks. Hey, Mom," I asked.

"Yes?"

"Have you ever been asked to keep a secret that you weren't sure was such a good idea?"

My mother, like a fighter pilot on target below her, zeroed in on my face. "No. Not really? Have you been asked to keep a secret?"

"Yes."

"What's the secret?"

I gave her an exasperated look I hadn't pulled out of the drawer since I was

21

sixteen. I had just told her it was a secret. I don't know why I was getting so upset about this. She was just asking questions. "It's a secret, Mother. I promised not to tell anyone."

"Well, it's obvious you need to talk about it." She led me over to the couch. "Sit down."

I followed her like a six-year-old.

"Whatever the secret is, just remember, if it's anything that endangers you or other people, you can't keep it. Do you understand that? Is there something about Ellie you need to tell me before the wedding? Is she, uh, in the family way?"

It amazed me she could write a romantic scene but couldn't say pregnant. "Of course not," I answered.

"That's a relief. Her mother would have been fit to be tied."

I stayed quiet. Holden's secret past could endanger Magnolia Daniels, but because I was so unsure what to do, I decided not to go any further.

"Well, whatever it is, just make sure you are doing the right thing, keeping this secret."

"You're right, and now that I've started talking about it, I realize I should keep it to myself. I'm sorry for worrying you." I stood to leave, feeling satisfied with my decision. If my mother became concerned, she would tell my father, who would then take it upon himself to try to "fix it."

"If you ever feel you need to break that secret, then please come to me. I would love to know what this is. It has nothing to do with Ben, does it?"

She had been changing the subject to Ben quite a bit lately. She wanted wedding bells going off for me as well as Ellie. She dropped a hint in nearly every conversation we had. Her generation was quick to marry, especially with the war going on. I knew I wasn't ready for that.

"Oh no. Nothing to do with Ben."

"Okay. Whatever you have going on, promise me you'll be careful. After what happened at Gibson Construction, I don't always trust your judgment."

Chapter Five

I eventually made it back to the radio station, where Holden expressed his gratitude for me accompanying his fiancée and mother to Bluebonnets. I gave him a brief report about the decision on the dress, and he seemed pleased.

I went to work while the resident cat, Uncle George, spread out in the beams of sunlight coming through the window. It wasn't long after that Leah came into the radio station and looked at the booth where Holden was working. "Thank you again for going with us this morning. I just know she made the right decision on the dress." She took her white gloves off finger by finger, getting frustrated as she completed the task. She obviously had something on her mind and wasn't the type of woman who had to wait for anything. "How long until there's a break?"

I checked the daily schedule. "It looks like he has ten minutes coming up when he plays the recorded news and weather." Holden made sure I had this scheduled every morning so that I wouldn't interrupt him when he was on the air.

"I'll wait." Leah nodded and sat down. "Planning a wedding is exhausting. Magnolia certainly seems to be very excited. I just wish her mother would have been there. Curious how she did not take part in choosing a wedding dress for her youngest daughter."

"Yes, I guess so, but not everybody enjoys planning this kind of thing. Have you ever met her?" My curiosity about Magnolia's mother was growing. Why was she absent from her daughter's life?

"Not yet. I do hope we'll get some time together before the wedding. It would be pretty awkward to be introduced at the reception." She let out her breath and folded her hands over her bag. I had the feeling she was working on containing her own opinion of Magnolia's mother.

Holden finished up what he was doing in the booth and opened the door. "Thanks for coming by, Mom. Come on in here."

Leah rose quickly, a look of concern on her face. "Yes, of course. I got your call. What happened?"

"Joyce Bishop happened. She called while you were at the dress shop. She is back at it since she saw the engagement picture in the paper. She came by the radio station telling everyone I killed Tracy. I can't believe this is happening right before Magnolia and I are to get married."

Leah turned around to close the door, but Holden stopped her. "It doesn't matter if the door is open or closed. Dot knows all about Joyce's accusations."

"That is very unfortunate," Leah said, her focus now turning to me. "I hope you will keep everything that you heard from that woman in the strictest of confidences. Holden is about to get married, and we want nothing to mess up our wedding schedule."

She turned back to Holden. "Does Magnolia know?"

"Not yet."

Once again, Leah addressed me, lifting her chin slightly. "Let's try to keep it that way, shall we? If news like this came out, the Daniels family could cancel the wedding. Accusations of murder do not play well in our circles."

As she said that, I debated whether Holden and his mother were actually a part of the Daniels' social circles. I held up my hand like I was taking a Girl Scout oath. "I do not plan to gossip about this." As I said it, I thought about my visit to my mother and how much I wanted to tell her. She was no dummy. She knew something was up. I could only hope I wasn't making a promise I would someday break.

Leah Ramsey scared me a little. She was in her early sixties, a faded beauty who looked formidable. I didn't think it would be healthy for me to cross her. Leah closed the door against her son's wishes. A request came with a phone call for "Chapel of Love" by the Dixie Cups. Fitting, when you considered how many people around me were getting married. When I hung up the phone, movement in the booth caught my eye. The discussion between Leah and her son had escalated. Their conversation had descended into a yelling match, and it was good that the booth was soundproofed. They weren't holding anything back. I looked at the clock and checked the schedule. Holden only had about a minute left. Even though I had been told that what Joyce Bishop had been saying was not true, the Ramseys almost acted like it was. Somehow, I felt there was a little smoke to go along with Joyce's fire.

After Leah left, Holden paced the floor of the booth between duties. Could he have been involved in the death of a young woman years ago? If he was, I could have the official title of working for the worst bosses in existence. I really liked this job. It was fun working in a radio station, and I enjoyed hearing music all day long, even if it was all 1950s ballads. Sometimes, recording artists even stopped by. Nobody really big, but it was exciting. They could be famous someday, and I could tell people I had met them at the beginning of their careers.

Whatever was going on, it couldn't be anything to worry about. I answered the phone for the rest of the afternoon and dealt with some typing and filing from our advertising clients. A record salesman in a wrinkled suit came in to pitch records to Holden. He called me baby, not something I was used to from a stranger, but that was the world of rock and roll music. Holden turned him away almost immediately.

Gerald turned back up again, ready to start his evening shift. He put his sack lunch down on my desk and gave me one of his bright white smiles. There was a warmness about him that made me instantly comfortable. He was only a couple of years older than I was and had gone to school in Camden. Unfortunately, even though the federal government issued a law to desegregate, Texas was choosing to do it year by year, starting with the elementary grades. We went to school in the same city, but on separate sides of town. I wondered if we would have been friends in high school.

I wanted to speak to him about his aspirations as a singer but didn't know where to start. I hummed along with the radio music coming over the loudspeaker. "I love this song. Do you sing?"

Gerald gave me a lopsided grin. "Yes. Yes, I do. I'm not church choir material, but I've sung along with Ray Charles records. Why do you ask?"

"I don't know. I thought that sheet music had to do with you wanting to be a singer. I'm sure a lot of disc jockeys also perform music."

Gerald put a hand on his chin. "I'm not the onstage type. I'd rather be doing just what I'm doing. Promoting the music, not playing." He glanced at the booth where Holden was setting up the next record. "I think Holden is the same way."

I really liked Gerald, but I couldn't stop thinking he was hiding something. His answers came too quickly sometimes. It was funny, but ever since this whole thing came out about Holden, I worried everyone around me was hiding some kind of secret. Gerald's secret had to do with that piece of sheet music, and I wasn't done asking questions about it. Until I could bring it up again, I changed the subject. "So, hear anything more about crazy claims on Holden? I guess Joyce called this morning. His mother came in, and they had a heated discussion over it."

"I'm sure they did. His mama is dead set on this wedding, and she will let nothing get in the way."

"I noticed that." Leah was the most involved mother of the groom I'd ever seen, and with Magnolia's absent parent, she seemed to take on the job of both mothers.

Gerald sat down in one of the lobby seats. "The way it usually works is some folks believe whatever lies and scandal people are talking about, from the line at the grocery store to the fellas sitting in the barber chair. It takes too much work to prove it otherwise, and those are the people you have to watch out for. You have to nip it in the bud."

When Gerald put it that way, I could understand such a clear view of the hazards of unproved gossip. I felt like there was something more there. "You sound like a man who has experience in this area. Don't tell me you've been accused of ending somebody's life."

Gerald shook his head, and I couldn't miss a hint of sadness in his eyes. "No, no. Not me. But my daddy was accused of something he didn't do. He ended up going to jail for it."

This was the first Gerald had told me about his family. "Really? What happened?"

He looked at his hands. "I don't talk about it too much because it makes me so angry. When I saw Joyce Bishop this morning, a lot of it came back to me."

"Why would Joyce trigger something like that?"

Gerald looked around, pressing his lips together. "Because it was her daddy who accused my daddy of stealing. It was a big fuss back then, and we went to court. You're a sweet kid, Dot, but you know, when you have a black man in court telling his side against a white man, it's easy to figure out which one the judge is going to believe, especially when the judge is also white. Wyatt Bishop said my daddy stole a car out of his garage, and it wasn't true. Daddy had nothing to do with that, and we came to find out later that Wyatt got drunk and crashed the car. He didn't want to tell his wife. So, instead of doing the right thing, he put Daddy in jail for three years for stealing a car. I don't want to have anything to do with that Bishop family because they're bad people. Joyce is no different from her daddy."

"But your dad didn't do it. Did they ever put Bishop in jail?"

Gerald's laugh became a snort. "Oh, you are an innocent."

I had no idea someone could just accuse you of a crime, and if your skin is not white, justice doesn't work for you. Truth, justice, and the American way, but Superman was white. Where was the justice for people like Gerald and his father? "What happened when they found out he was innocent? Did they let your father out?"

Gerald let out a soft laugh. "You'd think that would be what happened, but he was so near to the end of the sentence, they decided it wasn't worth it to let him out ahead of time. I'm sure they thought they were doing the community a favor by keeping him in jail as long as possible. Meanwhile, I lost three years of time with my daddy. He never got over that. None of us did. Still, though, my mama kept taking us to church every Sunday and told us to hold our heads up. The people in our church knew what happened wasn't true. They became the missing part of our family for a while."

"You think Joyce recognized you yesterday?"

"I'm sure of it."

"Did it make you angry when you saw her?"

"I'll admit it certainly didn't start my day out right. If I had it my way, my world would have absolutely no Bishops in it. That includes snippy daughters who make claims against my boss. He better watch himself because that family's good at taking people down. They certainly did it to us."

I wanted to say it might be different for Holden because he's white, but kept it to myself. I didn't have to tell him what he already knew.

Chapter Six

I looked forward to going out to dinner with my boyfriend Ben, a reporter for the *Camden Courier*. Even though Ben worked at a small newspaper, he fashioned himself quite the journalist, and really, he is. Ben and I started dating back in 1962, and I guess the town thinks we should be engaged, but I'm just not sure. I'd like to have a little more time on my own. It felt selfish to think about it, but Ben seemed happy with our situation.

We dined at Colombo's Italian restaurant that night. There are just a few restaurants in Camden, Texas, and Columbo's is one of our favorites. Joe Colombo, the proprietor, was like an uncle to me. Eating in his restaurant was like visiting his home with Dean Martin music on the stereo, the scent of a rich marinara sauce in the air. Sometimes, he would pour the entire restaurant a glass of wine to celebrate somebody's birthday. He had a heart for people and proved it as a member of the Camden City Council. As comfortable as I felt, what had happened at the office that morning was still on my mind. I felt like sharing it just to get it off my chest, but I had promised Leah Ramsey I'd keep it to myself.

Ben broke apart a breadstick, his gaze on me. "You seem distracted."

And I had thought I'd been doing such an excellent job of bottling it up. I put my hands on his. "Just tired."

"Okay. Are you sure there isn't something going on?"

There's only one problem with having a boyfriend who is a member of the media. I worried what I told him might end up in an article listing me as an anonymous source. He had promised me he would put nothing in print without my permission, but if the story was fantastic, how could he not? No.

I had to keep this to myself.

"Well, hello there." An older man with a lit cigarette, his silver hair brushed back in a pompadour and a silver mustache that reminded me of William Powell, extended his hand to Ben.

"Mr. Hill." Ben stood up and took his hand. "It's good to see you." From the adoring smile on Ben's face, I could tell he had great respect for this man.

The man smiled, making the crow's feet in the corner of his eyes grow deeper. "What's this 'Mr. Hill' business? I'm just like you, my man. Another reporter on the street with tired feet and a deadline to meet. Call me Nolan. We're not at the *Courier* right now."

Ben smiled, and as I watched him, I could see something in his eyes. Admiration. "Of course, Nolan. Won't you join us for dinner?"

Nolan Hill's eyes brightened. "I'd love to." After this, he finally made eye contact with me. "That is if I wouldn't be intruding. I wouldn't want to get between a fellow and his girl."

"Not at all," Ben assured him. It would have been nice if he had at least looked my way, but he didn't.

Nolan pulled out a chair and sat down. The waiter brought another place setting, and our new dinner guest put his cigarette on the saucer under his coffee cup. I appreciated that, because even though nobody else seemed to care about it, I had trouble eating in a restaurant filled with smoke. Before the waiter could leave, he caught his arm. "Bring me the veal piccata and whiskey, my man." He turned his hungry eyes to Ben. "How's it going, young buck? Any hot stories?"

Ben smiled and rubbed his hands together. "As a matter of fact, I'm on a pretty good one right now."

"Wonderful. You know, you're getting quite a reputation around the paper with your crime reports. I'm sure you're getting noticed elsewhere as well. Reminds me of my days when I was just a young cub reporter." His mustache twitched as he mentioned the word "reporter." It was obvious he relished the days he had left behind. Nolan had to be in his late sixties, well past the long days trudging to get a story.

"Are you retired?" I asked.

His neck stiffened slightly, and he changed his tone, speaking to me as you would a young child. "Legally, yes, I got my gold watch several years ago, but the heart and curiosity of a reporter never dies, young lady. We're always looking for that next big story."

"Absolutely," Ben confirmed, nodding his head up and down so quickly I worried about neck strain.

As I watched the two men, one young and one old, it was like traveling through time. Ben was the younger version of Nolan and probably how the old reporter still saw himself.

"Keep at it, my boy," Nolan said, his attention now fully directed back at Ben. "You're going places, but that only happens when you keep your nose to the grindstone."

"Actually, Nolan—"

There was a familiar giggle from across the room. Magnolia was out with Holden for dinner, and the two of them sat close together in the booth. He was running a finger across the top of her hand and whispering things in her ear. She seemed happy, which made me think she hadn't found out anything about Joyce Bishop's accusations. Ben's focus followed mine.

"Isn't that your boss?"

"Yes, and that's his fiancée," I answered.

"Oh. She's beautiful."

"Quite lovely. Who is she?" Nolan asked.

"That's Magnolia Daniels."

Nolan's eyes widened. "Oh, as in the 'oil wells' Daniels family? He certainly is hobnobbing with the upper class."

"The one and only."

Joe brought over two plates of Spaghetti Bolognese and Nolan's veal. Joe pinched his fingers together against his lips. "Bon appétit."

Nolan continued where we were before the plates arrived. "Yes, sir. The Daniels own a lot of property in this town. The last generation just kept making money. This one I haven't heard as much about. That happens sometimes in families. One generation is workers, and the next spends the money. Sad, really." Nolan raised his chin. "And the man there is your boss?

Where do you work?"

"KDUD."

"My favorite. You people know what kind of music to play. None of that rock and roll falderal. It's good to know your station has some standards." Nolan gave me an approving nod. I should have figured he would love listening to "Three Coins in the Fountain" all day.

Ben picked up his fork to twirl some spaghetti. "Interesting. I heard that the radio station was barely making it, but with the Daniels's money, Holden ought to sit pretty after this."

I was surprised by this news, but when I really thought about it, we always seemed to be on the hunt for new advertisers. "I didn't know the radio station was doing that badly."

Ben looked amazed. "Come on, Dot. The music he plays is so slow. With all due respect, Nolan, young people don't want to spend their days listening to "Autumn Leaves." They want the Beatles, Mary Wells, and The Beach Boys. If there's no audience, there are no advertisers. It works that way for newspapers, too. If there's no advertisers, there's no money."

As I processed what he was saying, a dull ache descended upon me. If there was no money, then there would be no job for me.

"Poppycock," Nolan protested. "There are many more of the older crowd in Camden."

"Yes, but do they buy the products advertised between the songs?" Ben asked.

There was a scuffle from behind us. Joyce Bishop was trying to make her way into the dining area, and Joe was attempting to hold her back. She quickly pushed past him.

"Ma'am, ma'am. Just wait here a moment, and I can offer you a table. Someone will be finished with their meal soon. Can I get you a drink at the bar?"

"I don't have to wait for a table. I know exactly where I'm going. I'm joining somebody."

Joe steepled his fingers, held them to his chest, and then nodded. "You just needed to say that, then. Please be my guest." He swished his hand over to the side, directing her into the restaurant. A dull ache formed in my temples, as I knew exactly where she was going. She stormed over to Holden's table.

"Magnolia Daniels?" Joyce said, a little louder than she should have been speaking.

Magnolia looked up with large brown eyes and gave a nervous smile. "Yes."

"Good. I need to talk to you. Do you realize your fiancé murdered a woman?"

Magnolia looked confused. "What?"

Holden stood up, throwing his napkin down on the table. "Joyce. You need to leave."

Joe placed himself behind Joyce, rubbing his hands together. "I am so sorry, Mr. Ramsey. She said she was invited to join your table."

"She was never invited to join us. This woman has been stalking me, and now she's trying to intrude on our dinner."

"I don't understand," Joe said. Magnolia's eyes were also full of questions.

Holden reached over and patted her hand. "It's really quite sad, but she fancies we once had a relationship."

"Sure. You were with me, and you were with Tracy. The only difference is I'm the one who survived. Tracy didn't. If Holden ever wants to go camping in the mountains, tell him no." Joyce stepped closer to Magnolia, then reached down and grabbed her shoulder. Magnolia tried to pull away, but Joyce wasn't having it. "I'm here to warn you. Your fiancé is not a good man. You could end up dead. Trust me. I know you think what I'm saying is crazy, but I'm here for your safety, that's all. I have about as much love for this guy as I do a box of cat litter."

Joyce's volume increased as Holden stood and pulled her away from Magnolia. He forcibly pushed her around, so she turned back to Magnolia and shouted. "Do you see? Do you see how he's treating me? I'm here to save your life. You need to stay away from him. He's already killed one girl, and you could be next." Her last words echoed across the now-silent diners as she was catapulted out the door by Holden and Joe.

Once she was outside, Joe stood at the door to make sure that she couldn't re-enter. Holden walked back into the dining room area. "Sorry, folks. That woman is not well. Please go back to your dinners." From the color on Holden's cheeks, I could tell he was extremely upset by Joyce's outburst. He quickly rejoined Magnolia, put both of his hands on hers, and whispered something we couldn't hear from our table.

But Magnolia was beyond soothing. "She's going to ruin it. She's going to ruin our wedding. I'm sure of it. It will all be spoiled."

Holden continued to try to calm her down, but she was hysterical.

Ben looked over at me in amazement. "What was that about? Did you know anything about this?"

I knew everything about it but was not prone to talk in front of two reporters.

Nolan looked like a bloodhound on the trail of a rabbit. "There's a story there someone needs to tell."

Now that everyone in Columbo's was talking about it, I guess my promise to Leah didn't matter anymore. The information was out, and I wasn't the one who spread it. "Promise me you won't put what I'm about to say in your paper with me as the source?"

Ben held up two fingers. "Scout's honor."

Nolan leaned forward. "Same here."

"She came to the radio station this morning." I briefly told them about the scene that played out and how I was told not to tell Magnolia.

Ben took a drink of wine. "Well, I guess she knows now. Amazing. I wish I had thought to bring my camera."

"Isn't that the way it goes for a journalist?" Nolan took a long drink of whiskey.

"This may make her call off the wedding," Ben said as he watched Magnolia, still upset.

"The rich hate scandals." Nolan tilted his head to the side as he watched the unhappy couple. "I would find it impossible for the Daniels to want to be associated with a past crime. Those nuptials are doomed."

I pushed back my plate, no longer hungry. "I hope not. Holden really loves her. Holden's mother asked me to keep it to myself. They really want nothing in the paper that might get back to the Daniels. Can you try to be objective about this?"

Nolan held up his whiskey glass for a refill. "That's hardly possible, young lady. There are too many witnesses to this incident to keep it out of the paper." Ben was still watching Holden's table. The whole restaurant was stealing glances at Magnolia and Holden.

"He's right. Everyone here saw what happened, Dot. We won't share what you just told us, but some of it has to come out."

"Well then, maybe mention a local disturbance, but be vague. No connection to Magnolia or Holden."

"Right. We can put it below the ball scores." He winked. "I might have to do a little better than that."

Once the waiter took Nolan's glass, he went back to cutting the veal on his plate. I had the feeling he'd put the story above the fold of the newspaper on the front page with one-inch lettering.

MURDER ACCUSATION RINGS THROUGH COLUMBO'S

Chapter Seven

The next day, I was back at my desk waiting for someone, anyone really, to ring the phone. I had caught up on the advertising work, and the request line was quiet.

After such a dull morning, it surprised me when the second line rang. We had both lines printed in the yellow pages, but most people used the first line. I punched the button, wondering how a song requester would know to use this line. "KDUD where the hits are playing." So not true, but that was what Holden paid me to say. It should have been KDUD, where the hits are missing.

"Could you play 'Love Me Do?' What do we have to do to hear the Beatles on the radio?"

"I'll put it on the DJ list. Thank you for calling KDUD." Holden playing the Beatles before noon would not happen, especially not when he was working his way through the hits of Mel Torme.

When the request line finally did ring, I jumped to answer it.

It was Ben on the line. "Hey, have you heard?"

I feared there was something further on the Magnolia situation. "Heard what?"

"They found a body over at the pet store."

"Really? At the pet store? I haven't been in there in years."

"You don't get it. The pet store is owned by the Bishop family. Joyce Bishop was found dead in the back room."

I gasped and then glanced over at the booth where Holden was in the middle of a long-winded story about how Frank Sinatra hated Marlon Brando in

Guys and Dolls. He called Brando "the mumbler" and was angry he didn't get the part in *On the Waterfront*. News of Joyce's death would come as a shock to Holden, and I couldn't deny it was awfully convenient.

"This is the same Joyce Bishop who's been accusing Holden of murder?"

"Yep. The same one."

I had never run into Joyce Bishop before, but now she kept popping up in my life.

Ben interrupted my thoughts. "Does Holden know?"

"I don't think so. I'm not sure how he'll take it."

I expected Ben to keep talking about Joyce, but there was a curious pause on the other end of the line. "So, Dot. I was wondering if you could help me with something."

I didn't like the sound of this.

"I need to get next to that crime scene, but I keep getting pushed back. Mary is already there as an investigating officer."

"She is? They let her go to a crime scene?" This was good news for my friend. She had to fight for every bit of actual police work she could get. Maybe things were loosening up in the old boys' club they called the Camden PD.

"Oh yeah, she's helping Detective Sprague. The problem is, I can't get past her. You know I wouldn't ask you this if I didn't absolutely have to, but I'm sure you could find out more about the crime from your old pal Mary. What do you say?"

Ben's request felt pushy. "I don't know if you've noticed this or not, but I have a job. I just can't go traipsing off to a crime scene. What happened is tragic, and it wouldn't be right to ask Mary to give you the inside scoop on it. Why are you even asking? She's going to say no. She's pretty adamant about not letting details concerning an ongoing case out to the press."

"I figured you'd say that, and we don't have to bug Mary, I promise. I have a way for you to be there and be doing your job. What do you think of that?" Ben desperately wanted to get this story. Nolan Hill's get-the-story-at-all-costs influence on him was changing him. He used to accept no for an answer.

"I think you're about to tell me."

"Go in and break the news to your boss. He will, of course, be sad, although the demise of Joyce Bishop, who's been spreading it around to anyone who will listen that he's a woman killer, is quite a motive. Offer to go there and look over the crime scene for him. You can promise to come back with a story for his news broadcast. Tell him you'll get an eyewitness story and give him the inside scoop on whether the police are looking at him as a suspect."

When he put it that way, it sounded like it might work. I was curious to see what had happened at the pet store, but I had never written a news story. I knew nothing about the who, what, when, where, and why. "I'm a secretary, not a journalist, remember?"

"I have faith in you. You were at the top of your class in secretarial school, and your ability to analyze a crime is excellent. Almost as good as mine."

"Laying it on a little thick, aren't you?" I paused for a second to think about it. Mostly, I wondered if Holden would go along with the idea. "Okay. I'll do it."

As I hung up the phone, I glanced at the DJ booth where Holden was writing notes while a record played. I still needed to deliver the Beatles request, so I used this as my opportunity to present him with the idea Ben had cooked up to get me to the pet shop.

"You got a request." I handed him the form. He barely looked up from what he was doing. Normally, I'd step back out of the room, so when I didn't, he stopped writing. "I was wondering if you'd heard the news about Joyce Bishop."

He scowled. "No. What has she done now?"

"It's not what she did, but what was done to her."

"What do you mean?"

I wasn't sure how to break this to him. He didn't seem to have any feelings for this woman, but he did in the past.

"She was found dead in the back of The Animal Kingdom Pet Shop. They think it was foul play."

Holden sat up, a confused look in his eyes. "Dead? What happened?"

"I'm not sure, but if you would like, I could go over and check it out.

38

My friend Mary Oliva, from the Camden PD, is there. She might tell me something, and I could even take some notes for the broadcast. They might even have a list of suspects."

Holden put his elbows on the desk, the weight of his chin in his palms. "I can't believe it. I just can't believe it. Joyce is dead." He lifted his chin. "Oh God. They might think I did it. Especially after she told the whole town, I killed my first wife."

"So, do you want me to go over there?"

He was staring forward with a vacant gaze, but then seemed to snap back. "Yes. I'd really appreciate it. I want to know what happened to her. Take notes, and I'll work it into a news report later. I want to know everything the police are thinking. Don't take too long though, because I need you on the phone."

"I'll be back in an hour."

Chapter Eight

When I met Ben at the pet shop a few minutes later, he stood with his hands in his pockets. The heat of May signaled the warming up in Texas, and he had foregone his traditional trench coat and now stood in a short sleeve white shirt and a thin black tie. Next to him was our dinner companion from the night before. Was Nolan Hill going to be accompanying us every time we were together now? I knew he inspired Ben to be a better reporter, but he wasn't doing much for me. It was obvious that he was living vicariously through Ben.

"How you doin' kid?" Nolan rubbed his hands together, looking like a man about to see a home run in the World Series. "Looks like we've got a hot one here." From what he described last night, I thought he retired. From his actions today, he was on the story.

"I'm surprised to see you here." I sidled up next to Ben, feeling a perverse need to claim ownership.

"Ben couldn't keep me away from this one," he answered.

"I'm just glad to have your expertise on the story," Ben said, then he drew closer to me. "I can't believe Holden went for you coming down here to report back. I should have known you'd find a way. Good old Dot."

That was me, good old Dot. Sometimes, I couldn't tell if we were friends or something more. I know I was being silly, but from our lack of physical closeness at times, I wondered if he was seeing other women. Maybe women he was much more involved with physically? Prior to this, I felt like what we had together was right for me, but now I wasn't so sure. I tried to slide those doubts into the background as I approached Mary, who was writing something down in a three-ring binder.

She looked up as I came closer. "I didn't expect to see you here," she said. She looked happy to see me right until Ben came up behind me. She slanted her eyes toward him. "I should have known he'd get you. I'm still not able to tell you anything about the crime scene, no matter who you drag down here."

"Would you mind repeating what you told Ben? Holden sent me here for the station news," I asked.

Mary nodded to the back room, and as I peered behind her, a crime photographer stepped into the doorway while taking a picture. There was blood on the floor, and I could just see Joyce Bishop's arm extended, her fingers slightly curled. Her skin was a grayish white, and her nails chipped. There was blood, lots of blood. So much so that as the smell drifted in our direction, I started moving back, feeling the contents of my stomach making its way up. Ben put his hand on my back to steady me.

I put my hand over my mouth and nose, trying to block the smell. I spoke through my hand. "Whoever did this was furious."

Ben didn't waste a moment and shot off a question to Mary. "Do you have any suspects?"

Mary let out an exasperated breath. "Ben Dalton. Stop being a reporter for a minute. If we just found a body, do you think I've got a list of suspects?"

"Actually, Holden wanted to know that too," I said.

"The public has a right to know," Nolan butted in, fury in his voice.

"I don't believe we've been introduced. Who are you?" Mary asked.

"Nolan Hill, reporter."

"Hmmm, I don't think I've seen you around before."

"Nolan is retired. He's helping Ben," I explained, but as I did, I couldn't help noticing the surly gaze Nolan gave me. He didn't want anyone thinking he was anything but on the job.

Mary crossed her arms. Nolan Hill might be a hard-core journalist, but he had just met his match. Not only was she an excellent cop, but she was also a mother. She knew how to set things straight with just a few words. "Well, Mr. Hill, the public does have a right to know the facts, and it's our job to make sure that the correct information gets out to them."

Ben cut back into the conversation. "So, when do you think it happened?"

A detective walked behind Mary, and I couldn't help noticing he left a trail of blood on the floor with his shoes. Mary spoke. "Last night, I guess."

"Uh, Mary. That guy is tracking blood all over the crime scene."

Mary looked back. "Hey, Peterson. Watch where you're steppin.'" The man stopped.

"Damn," said another cop. "Peterson, you need to point out where've you've been. What are you, an idiot?" I recognized this guy as Detective Sprague. "Good catch, Officer Oliva."

"Yes, sir," she responded and then whispered in my direction, "Thanks, Dot."

"Glad to help." We shared a grin. It was hard for Mary to get noticed in a department full of men. "I guess you heard there was a big dust-up with her at Columbo's last night," I said.

Mary turned a shoulder to Ben and Nolan and focused on me. "No. What happened?"

"She came in saying Holden had killed his first wife and wanted to make sure Magnolia knew about it. She'd tried the day before at the radio station, but just missed her. She wanted to warn her."

"That's interesting. " She pulled up the binder again.

Ben continued the story. "It was a big scene, and Joe had to take her out of the restaurant."

"I would say you have two easy suspects there, Missy," Nolan added.

Mary wrote some of our conversation. "That's Officer Oliva to you, Mr. Hill. So, how did Magnolia take it?"

"As well as any girl would take it after finding out the love of her life may or may not be a murderer. She was upset," Ben said.

"Good to know." Mary finished writing and closed the binder.

"I think I've given you more information than you've given me. Let's even that up." Ben leaned forward slightly to make up for the difference in their height. He was shadowed by Nolan, who also leaned. "Anything else you'd like to share with the *Camden Courier*?"

"No comment, and quit your complaining. You have more facts than you did. I'd say we're even already." Mary scowled at Ben and gave a particular look of distaste to Nolan. I knew she hated saying anything to the press and might have to answer to the chief if too much got out. They were already looking for ways to keep Mary in the filing room. Men loved to complain about how women talked too much.

Chapter Nine

When I returned to work, I gave a quick report to Holden about what I had witnessed at the crime scene.

"Thanks for doing that. I'm relieved to hear they don't have me on the suspect list yet. Write it up for me, okay?" His face was grim, and I had to consider that as big of a pain Joyce was, he had dated her once. When had Joyce found out about Tracy? Was that what broke them up, or had they been heading that way? I found it interesting that the Bishops, although not as well off as the Daniels, also had property in town. I think Holden's type was a girl with family money. Joyce wasn't half as attractive as Magnolia was, but Holden got lucky with that. If the radio station was in the red, then maybe marrying into deep pockets would be the answer to save it.

I had volunteered for the job of reporting on the crime scene but dreaded writing out what I had witnessed. Joyce, lying there dead, shook me in a way I hadn't realized. She had been so alive just hours before, but now the puddles of blood kept coming back to me. There had been a smear of blood on a white Frigidaire, probably where Joyce had struggled against her attacker before she fell. How could Mary stand seeing murdered people? As I tried to get back to work, thankfully, the phone rang.

"Yes, I have a request." It sounded like an older lady with a very low voice. Probably a smoker. "I would like to hear that nice boy, Tony Bennett."

"Certainly. I'll get your request to the DJ."

"Thank you, dearie. I was listening to the top hits at KOOL, but I'd much rather hear all the tired old songs you play. It really soups up my Geritol."

"Great. I'll make sure we play some Tony Bennett."

Suddenly, the voice on the other side changed. "That's right, ladies and gentlemen. Go to KDUD as in 'dud' if you want to fall asleep at seven o'clock in the evening like your grandma, but KOOL will keep you up and dancing." It was the DJ at KOOL, and I was pretty sure we were on the air. He hung up. This was the second call I'd received like this in a week. I was tempted to call him back, but why bother? I wouldn't be on the air for everyone to hear him make fun of me again.

It was about an hour later when Leah came storming into the radio station and trailing behind was her assistant, Morris. He had been with her on several visits, and he seemed more like a friend than a servant. He stood with his cap in his hands. His thinning hair was strawberry blond, and his weak chin sunk into his neck when he looked down. He was a man in his early fifties, slightly pudgy with a subservient air to him.

Leah did not look happy. "Hello, Dot. Go give my son a note that I need to speak with him."

"Sure." I pulled a piece of paper from my message pad.

"Better yet, I'll just step in myself and wait for him. I can see you're busy here."

She turned to Morris. "You wait here. I won't be too long."

Morris nodded. A strand of his straight, thin red hair fell on his round forehead. "Yes, ma'am. I'll be right here. Take your time."

Leah opened the door to the DJ booth and held one finger against her lips. Holden looked up, his hand on his headset. Amazingly, if you were listening to him, you wouldn't know someone had just walked in. He never lost his on-air banter.

"Let's all start dancing around with a little 'Singing in the Rain.' Hope you brought your umbrella." He put the record on, then pushed a couple of buttons to mute the microphone. He turned to his mother, who had left the door partly open, so this time I could hear them.

"I figured you'd be here."

"Well, we have to discuss this." As Leah finished her sentence, she turned around and gently closed the door. So much for getting to listen in.

Morris had settled into a chair. When I looked his way, he gave me a close-lipped smile.

"Can I get you some coffee?" I asked. Even though I worked in the radio station lobby, most of the time, I was the only one there. Morris sitting there staring in my direction made me feel uncomfortable. He shook his head no, the quiet smile still plastered on his face.

"Your boss is pretty upset," I said.

Instead of answering me eye to eye, he shifted his focus to the rim of his green plaid cap. "Oh yes. It's to be expected with all this nonsense going on. Mrs. Ramsey is a strong woman, a brave woman. She'll sort it out." His admiration of Holden's mother rang through his words.

"I guess you would know more than anybody. How many years have you worked for Mrs. Ramsey?"

"She hired me shortly before her husband died. She needed me to take up some duties that he did around the house, and that's what I do. The garden, handyman work, driving her around. Mrs. Ramsey doesn't drive."

That was surprising because most of the women I knew in 1964 had a driver's license, but it spoke back to the one-car-per-family times in the '40s and 50s. Lately, I'd heard some families were buying two cars because women were working outside the home more. Mary and John Oliva were a prime example of this.

A clatter came up behind us, and I realized that Leah and Holden were once again having an argument. So much for mother-son bonding.

The door opened abruptly. "I need you to go, Mother. We can discuss this later. I can't have this conversation while I'm trying to work."

Leah pleaded. "You must understand. This can ruin everything."

"I understand perfectly, but this is neither the time nor the place to deal with this."

Leah clenched her fists. "This wedding is very important, and we will need her family support, both financially and socially. If we can keep this quiet, that's fine. But now that Joyce has died, I don't know if we can. What if the newspaper were to pick up Joyce's obsession with your first wife?"

"Now you're being silly. I don't think the local press is smart enough to come up with a conspiracy theory. They'll focus on the intruder that killed

Joyce. They won't waste time learning about her. She's a pet store employee. Not too exciting."

Leah's eyes closed to the tiny space of slits. "Fine. If Magnolia asks about Joyce, just tell her what an awful shame it is and change the subject."

"I'm handling it, mother." She stepped out of the booth quietly and closed the door.

"I'm ready to go home now, Morris."

Morris put his cap back on. "Yes, ma'am."

Chapter Ten

Holden was animated on the air after his mother left, but in the downtime, I noticed him sitting with his elbows on the counter. The front he put on while broadcasting was easy-going and happy, but his true self showed up in those moments. When I first arrived at KDUD, I didn't know about the history of the station. It had been on the air around my parents' home while growing up, and I associated it with songs from ten years ago. They put in the recording studio in the back of the station to do a live church performance with gospel music on the radio every Sunday morning. The Schulz family owned it, and then, when Wedge Schulz died, the gospel broadcasts stopped. That's where I lost track.

According to Gerald, there was another owner in between who went belly up within a year. He priced the studio low for a quick sale, and that was when the Ramseys showed up with a down payment and Holden's dream of being a DJ.

They kept costs at a bare minimum with a small staff. Now, with the rumors swirling around Joyce Bishop's murder, this wouldn't help sales.

I couldn't deny that I was feeling some genuine friendship for Holden, mostly because he was so nice most of the time. He made me feel special when he talked to me, almost to the point of flirting. It was such a stark contrast from my last boss, who loved to belittle everything I did. It was nice to come to work and be around this pleasant, attractive man. Yes, he was older than I was, but he was very handsome in a mature way. His hair was salt and pepper, and his jawline was strong, reminding me of William Holden. Younger women and older men were easily accepted by our society, not that I was ever thinking about doing that. Magnolia had to be ten or fifteen years younger than he was, but he was still so charismatic that he could attract a woman like that.

I poured Holden a cup of coffee and walked into the DJ booth.

"How are you doing?"

"You must be reading my mind." He took the cup. "I don't know what I was thinking of trying to keep my past from Magnolia. What happened was an accident. Even the police said so, but it feels like I'm being tried for murder, even though I've never been charged with anything."

"If I'm not being too nosy, how did Joyce know about this?"

"She had a very reliable source. I told her. We had a little too much to drink one night, and I told her everything. She seemed okay with it for a while. Then I found out that she had been at the library looking up newspaper articles about Tracy and her death."

"How did you find out?"

"I found a notebook hidden in a drawer behind the counter at the pet store. She had been taking notes on the newspaper articles and listing them. She always was a talented student, and it was like she was writing some sort of research paper on the whole incident."

"Can I ask just what happened to your first wife? I mean, if it's not too painful."

His mouth lifted into a sweet smile, and he ran his hands through his hair. "I guess you're going to find out, eventually. We were hiking in Colorado. She loved to hike. She loved anything outdoors. She wanted me to take her picture, so I went to the car to get my camera as she was trying to situate herself on the edge of the cliff at the lookout. When I came back, she was no longer there. She lost her footing and fell to her death. It was ruled an accident."

"So why was Joyce so sure you did something criminal?"

"I guess it frightened her. We were never the same after that night. It's what broke us up. Joyce told her pastor, Rob Roy, at Living Word, and he went to the police. I guess the confessional creed only works for the person doing the confession. Second-hand wicked deeds can be announced anywhere.

I was questioned in Colorado, mostly for the police to get an idea of what happened. It was ruled an accident. Joyce couldn't accept it. She was never one to shy away from sharing her opinion. It didn't make things easy between her and mother, either."

After seeing Joyce's behavior in the station, this made perfect sense. Could her assertiveness make enemies in other situations? "Do you know anybody who would want to kill Joyce?"

He cued up a record. "You mean besides me? Who knows? She was like a dog with a bone. Once she had an issue, she just couldn't let it go. I can only hope she had some other ex-boyfriend that she was hounding about something. I don't know what I ever saw in her."

Holden was like a man who kept trying to restart his life while bad luck hung over him like a storm cloud. "For what it's worth, I believe you, and I'm so sorry this has happened to you."

He turned to me and then placed his hand over mine. This simple gesture made a warmth spread through me. "I really appreciate that." There was a silence between us, but not an uncomfortable one. More like the building of trust and then something else. The very thing that seemed to be missing between me and Ben right now.

As seductive as it was, it wasn't right. "I better get back out there. I'm sure someone is going to call to request 'Love Me Do.' It's been very popular all day, and I don't think you played it at the last request."

He pulled his earphones back up and turned his attention to where the needle was on the record.

As I stood in the lobby, I realized something. I was developing feelings for Holden.

Chapter Eleven

fter finding out Joyce talked to her pastor, I visited the Living Word Church. I hoped my visit would give me a clue to whoever had killed her. If I could figure that out then maybe I could bring some relief to Holden and Magnolia. There was going to be a Wednesday night service, and I planned to catch him after church to see if he might offer insight on what Joyce had shared with him. A pastor might give me an unbiased opinion of her accusations against Holden.

I showed up near the end of Pastor Rob Roy Ferguson's sermon.

"And so, I say, brothers and sisters, you need not look for sinners in the world; you just need to look to yourself. Bring up that mirror and take a long, hard look." He raised his finger and then scanned the room with it as if pointing to every individual parishioner who sat rapt in attention to his words. His gaze lit on me and then he pointed, making me squirm in my seat. "None of you is without sin. None of you. Remember that and repent because surely goodness and mercy will follow you for the days of your life. Amen." The crowd corresponded with a hearty "Amen." A hymn started, the offering basket went around, and the service quickly finished up. I waited until most of the congregation had gone through the handshaking line, continually letting other people step in front of me. When there was no one else left, I walked over to the pastor.

He shook my hand, his gaze curious. "You are new to our flock."

"I was actually here so I could talk to you about something."

"Of course, sister. Whatever's on your mind, you've come to the right place. This is God's house." He let go of my hand and put both hands up. "This is your house. Be at home here."

"I wanted to ask you some questions about Joyce Bishop."

He brought his arms down, and his focus turned back to me so abruptly it was unnerving. "Such a terrible tragedy. Joyce was a member of our congregation."

"Yes, I know. I work with Holden Ramsey, and she came into our office the day before she was killed. She was extremely upset about him being engaged to Magnolia Daniels. She kept talking about how his first wife died. Holden told me she also shared this with you, and I was wondering if there was anything you'd be comfortable telling me about your time with her."

A change came into the pastor's eyes. He looked from side to side as if checking to see if anybody else was listening to us.

"Well, I like to keep pastoral conferences confidential, but I can tell you she was mighty upset about the death of that poor woman in Colorado. She shared that with others besides myself, so I'm not completely breaking a confidence."

"Did she accuse Holden of killing her?"

"Oh yes, yes, she did. I have to tell you I've worked with members of my congregation for decades, and well, I don't want to sound terrible, but this seemed to come under the title of female hysterics. Sometimes, the fairer sex can be excitable." He said it as if a member of the fairer sex were not standing in front of him. "Joyce was terribly wound up and distraught over the whole thing. Out of fairness to her, I reported our counseling session to the local police even though it was technically out of their jurisdiction. That was the only way I could get her to stop talking about it. That seemed to satisfy her. As you know, it didn't go any further than that."

"Holden told me that. So, you think she was hysterical?"

"Oh yes, many of our single sisters tend toward high emotions." He gave me a fatherly smile. "That's why they need to have a good man in their lives. Someone to keep them settled down." I couldn't help but notice he had glanced at my left hand before he made his last statement. Why did I suddenly feel in his perceptions of me, he was saying to himself, *This woman needs a man.*

"Thanks for your help, pastor." I quickly ended our conversation. The one person Joyce consulted to get help had characterized her as hysterical. No wonder she blew up at the radio station.

When I got home from the church, I found a note on the counter. Ellie and Al were going out to see *Viva Las Vegas* at the Rialto. It was a brand new movie, and everyone in town wanted to see it. Ben was meeting them there as well. She wanted to meet before the movie to discuss wedding plans. The movie started in half an hour. Ellie had been so emotional lately. I was leery of what she wanted to talk about. At least the movie theater had Milk Duds. That would help.

Before I could get out the door, the phone rang.

"Dot, it's your mother." As if I wouldn't recognize her voice immediately.

"Hey, Mom. I was just on my way out the door. Is everything okay?"

"Oh, yes. I'm sorry. I shouldn't have bothered you."

Guilt washed through me. "No, I've got a minute. What did you need?"

There was a pause at the other end, and I heard my mother take a breath. "Good. I was just wondering, well..."

"Yes?" I really only did have a minute, but it was clear she was having trouble using this time appropriately.

"Don't laugh, okay?"

"Promise." I looked at my watch.

"You read some of my book when you visited the house, and well, I rewrote the line you were reading about the girl finding the man in the hayloft."

That explained why she was nervous. "Sure. It was, uh, great." I wish I really felt that way, but the thought of my mother writing romance was a little creepy.

"Thank you. That means a lot to me. What you read was a first draft, and I felt it lacked something, you know? I've rewritten that line with a little more intrigue in it. Do you want to hear it?"

"Sure." Especially if this would end the conversation and get me out the door.

"Great. Here goes."

Felicia walked into the barn and there she saw the burly shoulders of Jacob as he

53

hefted the hay into the hayloft. He turned to look at her, a heat smoldering deep into his eyes. A thrill ran through her. Was it passion or fear? She caught her breath as her bosom heaved upward. He was her everything.

The passage had taken on a darker tone. Now this romance was beginning to sound interesting, even if it was being written by my mother.

"I like it."

"You do? Oh, thank you so much for listening. I'll keep working on it. Now you be on your way. You don't want to be late."

When I walked up to the theater, Ellie, Al, and Ben were all sitting outside on the concrete flower box, sharing a carton of Good & Plenty Licorice candies. Ellie was speaking with great animation while Al was shaking his head no, his cheeks full of candy.

These two needed to get married soon, because the pre-wedding drama was driving us all crazy. On top of that, she was putting off making her own wedding dress.

"You made it. " Ben stood up and kissed my cheek. "Where were you?"

"I was at church. "

Ben looked surprised, but Ellie, who had been engaged in conversation with Al, looked shocked.

"At church? Tonight?"

"I wanted to talk to somebody, and so I went to the church where I knew they would be."

"That's interesting." Ben slid his arm around my shoulder. "Anything we can do? Who did you want to see?"

"It's not important. I'll talk to you about it later." I turned my attention to Ellie. "I've been dying to see this movie, but why the big meeting before?"

"I just wanted to discuss something with all of you. Because you're the maid of honor and Ben is the best man, I wanted you to know that I'm thinking about making some changes to the wedding." My gaze drifted to Al, who seemed to be very busy trying to close the empty box of candy.

"What would you think—" Ellie raised her voice in excitement. "—If we eloped? "

And there was the reason I wanted my cousin to hurry and get married.

One week she didn't want to get married, and the next, she was doing her own version of *Viva Las Vegas*. "You want to elope now?"

"Yes!" She clapped her hands together and did a little jig, making the theatergoers give her a second look. Ellie was always big on ideas, practical or not.

I tried to speak calmly, hoping to settle her down before we all hopped in the car to wake up a justice of the peace. "Ellie, I don't understand. You've been planning this wedding for the last year. Shoot. You've been planning this wedding for your entire life. Why would you want to elope now?"

Al finally spoke up. "Exactly. Listen to your cousin, Ellie." I was wondering when he would become a part of this conversation.

Ellie knocked her head back slightly and took a breath. She looked annoyed at having to explain her need to elope. "But I'm in the wedding business. I've been to more weddings than anyone I know, and so the whole stressful production with the bride and the groom, and the church, and the dress, and the cake, is just not necessary for me and Al. Look at us. We're mature individuals."

"Think about it, Ellie," Ben said. "That's all the more reason to have a real wedding."

I loved my cousin, but she was cracking under the strain, and it became more evident with every second that went by. "I think you're overwhelmed right now. Don't shortchange yourself out of your wedding just because it feels like such a mountain to climb. Please reconsider this. What about your dress? I think it would be a great way to really show what you've got on the design side."

"I don't care."

Al held his hands up in frustration. "But you have a dress, right?"

"I'm busy." Ellie crossed her arms in front of her slim figure. "It's wedding season."

"Ah, I don't want to hear it." With that, Al walked away and went to the ticket booth, pulling out his wallet.

"Listen, Ellie. It's time to hire someone to work in the store. If you won't do that, then the problems you're facing are problems that you've created.

Not doing anything is as bad as making a wrong decision. I heard that Mrs. Reynolds needs money after her husband died in the oil field. She has four kids to raise. I'll bet she'll help you in a heartbeat, especially if she can work on the sewing at her house. Not only would you be helping yourself, but you'd be helping her."

Al came back with the tickets and handed two to Ben. "I want to marry you like crazy, Ellie, but lately, you're more than this old boy can handle. I'll do whatever you want, but time is running out." He turned to Ben. "I think I'd rather walk in with you right now." He crooked his arm, and Ben laughed and stuck his hand in it.

"Shall we?"

Ben smiled. "Of course."

Ellie scowled. "Great. The clock's ticking, and he's skipping into the movie with your boyfriend."

"He just wants you to decide, Ellie. You're so close. It's like you don't want to get to the finish line. You're self-sabotaging."

"I am not."

"I think you are."

As we walked in, Al and Ben were standing by the door of the auditorium. I gladly took Ben's hand, and then he squeezed it, and I noticed he had a ridiculous smile on his face. "What's going on?"

"Not much." He practically sang his words to me. "It's just that—" He drew closer. "I got a job offer today."

"Don't you already have a job?" We sat down in a row near the front, next to Al and Ellie.

"I do, but this job would be at the *Dallas Morning News*. They want me to come on board and help with the crime report. They've been reading some of the stories I wrote about the crimes here in Camden."

"That's wonderful." I grabbed his face and kissed him.

"Now I can see there are some added benefits to this job." He bobbed his eyebrows at me.

"That's amazing," Ellie said. "Are you considering doing this?"

"Oh yes. This is why I got into journalism."

Al leaned forward. "Doesn't that mean you'll have to work in Dallas?"

"Yes," Ben stated flatly. "I have a new job. I'll be moving away."

He said it so easily. He had made this decision and hadn't even consulted me? Was I not important enough to him to be a part of his future? My earlier fears crept back into my thinking. Could there be other women in his life? "I see." A coldness came over me as I leaned away from Ben.

"I'll be back whenever I can." Ben reached over and attempted to pull me back. The cartoon was coming on, and the carousel-sounding music made the moment even more absurd. "You have to understand, Dot, I can't pass up an opportunity like this."

"I understand. Sure." It took everything I had to lighten up my voice. "After all, we're just having fun, you and me. It's not like we're engaged or anything. It's the swinging sixties, right?" I let out a shallow laugh that hit right before Bugs Bunny clobbered Elmer Fudd with a wood mallet on the theater screen.

"Yeah." Ben sounded relieved. I guessed I fooled at least one person. "It's not like we're engaged or something. I am going to miss you a lot. A lot." He looked over at Al and Ellie. "Anyone else want popcorn? I'm heading to the snack bar."

After getting an order for a large butter tub from Ellie, he sauntered up the aisle, and why not? He had a new job offer and would be shedding the little town of Camden for the bright lights of the big city.

I had taken what Ben and I had for granted. You never know you're going to miss something until you no longer have it. I had purposely not progressed our relationship because I just felt like there was so much of my life that I wanted to live. Yes, we had been dating for over a year, but I was okay with that. Now, with the thought of him moving to another city, a big city filled with beautiful women, a little tap of panic started playing its drum in the back of my mind. Ben was leaving. I reflected on Pastor Rob Roy's words about how women needed men in their lives, and the entire statement made me furious. Some feminist I was. I was falling into the stereotype by mourning a loss that hadn't even happened. I just couldn't make myself believe the pastor was correct in his assumptions about women and their place in the world. If Ben wanted to go, fine. I needed to keep telling myself that.

Chapter Twelve

I couldn't shake the mood the next morning from my movie date with Ben. I really liked that gangly reporter who could make me laugh and always made me feel safe. Maybe I even loved him, but the next step was really scary for me. I was now beginning to think I'd moved too slowly. It seemed like in the movies, the couple always fell in love so fast. In real life, the days and nights of living get in the way of the fluidity. At least, that was what was happening with me. I wanted to be around Ben, and I loved it when we kissed. He had always been a perfect gentleman, even on the nights when I was sure I could go farther. Just my luck. Trying to clear my worries, I mindlessly took calls and relayed music requests, but I never felt that element of fun I had before working at the radio station. Uncle George sat on the edge of my desk, purring and licking his paws. It was almost as if I could see a concerned look in his eyes, but then I decided I would welcome anything that even remotely felt like solace.

I was taking another request call when a low, gravelly voice on the other end of the line asked for Gerald.

"He comes in at night. Can I take a message for him?"

"Yeah. We need to know about what time we should come in." I rarely booked appointments for Gerald on the graveyard shift, but I took the message, anyway. I'd have to ask him who the man with the gravelly voice was. Sometimes we had singers or even entire groups come in to sing over the radio, but Holden handled all of that.

It was about 10:00 a.m. when Magnolia called.

"Dot, I'm in a bit of a pickle, and I was wondering if I could ask you a big favor."

From being around her for the last six months, I recognized she was putting on her sweetest voice. "First, I am furious with the girl that I asked to be my maid of honor. We had been in school together since kindergarten, and she was my ideal choice for maid of honor, but since the Joyce Bishop story came out, she no longer wants to be involved with the wedding. Can you believe it?"

Could it be that some people who ran in Magnolia's social circle were not genuine friends but props in the ideal life of the social elite? Magnolia was now in the category of people they might not deem worthy because of her involvement in such a nasty scandal.

"Anyway, I'm about to talk to Holden about this, but I'll need you to come to my house to meet my mother."

"Why do I need to meet your mother?"

"Oh, I forgot to actually ask you. Will you fill in for my maid of honor?"

Magnolia had just gracefully delivered a backhanded compliment. I wasn't her maid of honor. I was her fill-in.

"My mother is pretty picky about who's going to be in the wedding, and well, she doesn't know you."

"Why do you think I'd be acceptable as your maid of honor? I'm your fiancé's secretary."

"Oh, don't be silly, of course, you're good enough to be in my wedding. You are good enough for my future husband to hire, right?"

No matter how she tried to put it, I was still a poor second for a replacement. There was no way her mother was going to take to me, but I wasn't sure how I could bow out of the commitment.

"What time can you come over and meet my mother?"

"I don't know. I mean, I'm honored." Sort of, I thought. "But you should talk to Holden and see what he says." I transferred the call over to Holden in the booth before she could say anything else. He was rubbing at his temples. Weddings were hell on people. I saw it happen with Al and Ellie, and now with Holden and Magnolia. That whole idea of eloping to Las Vegas was pretty enticing for couples at this point. No fuss, no muss, you're married.

I often wondered if brides who married quickly like that came to regret it years later. I think I would because I also have always dreamed of a beautiful wedding. I was seeing the stress that mounted in the months before the actual occasion was something else altogether. Everybody dreams of a beautiful wedding, but what they don't tell the bride is she's the one who has to pull all this magic off, and it isn't easy. At the next commercial break, Holden came out of the DJ booth.

"We really want to thank you for agreeing to be our maid of honor."

Funny, but I never recalled saying yes. I was simply a part of the plan. A prop to be moved around in Magnolia's stylish wedding.

"I don't know if this is such a good idea."

"I know. Her mother is exceedingly difficult to work with, so instead, we thought it might be good before you go over there to stop by my mother's house. You can look at the bridesmaid's dress, and the three of you can call Magnolia's mother. We really appreciate you stepping in like this."

Against my better judgment, I drove over to Leah Ramsey's house and Holden's present home. Morris was out trimming the bushes while Leah sat at a patio table drinking lemonade. "You made it. That's good, because we have a lot to do, and we can't afford to waste any more time on fickle maids of honor. I certainly hope you won't be that way."

Morris came forward with the clippers in his hands. "Now, Mrs. Ramsey. We don't want to run this one off too, now do we?" He gave me a little smile with a twinkle in his eyes. At least I had one person who saw me as more than a stand-in bridesmaid.

A softness came over Leah Ramsey's face, and she spoke this time with a much less commanding tone. "Of course, Morris. You're right. It's just that we want everything to be perfect for the wedding, and a last-minute replacement is just what every bride doesn't want to experience."

"I'm here. I'm here." Magnolia ran up with shopping bags over each arm. "I found the best sale over at Dillard's, and I just had to pick up every single one of them they had. She pulled out a box of white ladies' gloves. "Aren't they just adorable? They'll look so good coming down the aisle."

Leah's mouth scrunched into a downward angle. "White gloves? Personally,

I love to wear them. I think they delineate social class, but really? Do they wear white gloves at weddings in this day and age?"

"Both of my sisters had white gloves at their weddings, and I just thought it would be a wonderful addition to what's already happened in our family. Don't you agree, Dot?"

"I guess so." My enthusiasm for wearing white gloves did not come through as authentic. White gloves were from the 1950s. The next thing she would want us to wear full skirts with petticoats and a poodle or two on the bottom.

"Tradition is huge with my family, and if I want them all to be happy, I'm just trying to find a nice middle ground with them. You understand that, don't you?" Magnolia began putting her fingers one by one into a soft white glove.

Morris came forward again. "I think they are lovely, Miss Magnolia. Your mother will be thrilled."

Magnolia gave Morris a hug. "I knew I could count on you, Morris."

He had a way of smoothing things over. I guess I could wear a pair of white gloves for a few hours. I just hoped they weren't serving crawfish.

"I want to make doubly sure that the band that I booked will be there."

"Who did you book?" Leah asked, taking a sip of her lemonade as a slight breeze blew across all of us.

"Oh, they're the best. They're called The Harmony Kings. I heard them at a club before Holden, and I started dating. I've tried to get him there, but he always finds a reason to go somewhere else. I just love their music."

"The Harmony Kings? That sounds interesting. What kind of music do they play?"

"They do some rock and roll and some ballads, you know, music you can dance to," Magnolia said.

Leah crossed her legs and straightened her back. She gave Magnolia a withering look. "Also, the type of music that your mother will not like. Are you sure you want to go that far with this band?"

"Yes. Did you know when Gerald isn't working at the radio station, he's kind of like a what do they call that, a promoter. When I said I might be interested in them for the wedding, he actually helped me to talk to the leader of the band. Isn't that great?"

This was interesting news about Gerald. I thought all he did was work at the radio station at night, but here was proof that he was working as a music promoter. It also added more mystery to the gravelly voice. Magnolia continued talking.

"Yes, and the leader of the band has this low, low voice. It's really quite sexy."

Leah sat up. "Oh really, Magnolia, sexy? You are an engaged woman, and this man is…is…colored, is he not?"

Magnolia didn't seem to be concerned with Leah's disapproval and kept talking. "And then he has this cute way of ending all of his sentences with darling. He sure isn't Perry Como, that's for sure. That man has more heat than Perry Como would have sitting on the furnace."

Why was it that this description of the leader of The Harmony Kings sounded so much like the gentleman who had called me on the phone looking for Gerald? Could it be the same man, and just how much was Gerald doing on the side? I needed to talk to him because I really liked Gerald and didn't want him to get in trouble.

Leah rose. "Shall we call your mother and tell her about Dot now?"

Magnolia put the gloves back into the bag. "I've already told her. She's in one of her…moods, so let's not bother her. It's sweet of you to try to help, but it's been taken care of."

When I returned to the station, I still hadn't had the chance to talk to Holden about my visit to Joyce's pastor, but Holden was busy with a new promotion. Joyce Bishop had just been found murdered, but at KDUD, life was moving on.

I entered quietly and stood in the booth, but again, he didn't look up. Finally, I said, "I have some news about Joyce."

"I love it that you're being helpful, Dot, but not now. Magnolia wanted me to pick the music for the wedding. I think I came up with a pretty boffo list. I know it's going outside of your job duties, but if I don't get this promo package finished, we won't be able to launch it on time. Magnolia is back home, and I know I just sent you out to my mother's house, but could you run these over to Magnolia's house? It will give her mother a chance to meet you now, anyway. I promise, as soon as all this wedding nonsense is over, all you'll have to do is answer the phone." Holden Ramsey had a look to him that was hard to resist. He reminded me of Bobby Kennedy. So much boyish charm.

I gave in. "If you can handle the phone lines, it's no problem."

He reached over and, to my surprise, he grabbed my hand and then gently kissed it. "Thank you so much, my dear. What would I do without you?" Releasing me, he handed me a stack of 45s and a handwritten list of songs.

I backed out of the booth, feeling confused about that kiss. The confusion was possibly because of my boyfriend announcing he was going to be moving to another city to take a new job. How could Ben not talk to me about a major move? I thought we were close, but maybe my feelings were one-sided. I had to think Holden would have asked me first.

Ten minutes later, I was knocking on the door of the Daniels' home. This house was in the King's Hill neighborhood, the nicest place to live in Camden. It was intricately landscaped with precise tiny bushes encircling a golden and white fountain with streams of water tastefully flowing into concrete clamshells built into the rim. It was set in the middle of a circular drive, which showcased the house. I counted four gables, and the front opening was a cool respite from the stuffiness of May in Texas. I knocked several times on the heavy oak door until a woman answered, wearing large tortoiseshell sunglasses and holding a lit cigarette in her hand. She looked like she was about to go out somewhere as she positioned a scarf around her neck.

"Yes?" Her tone was somewhere between annoyed and dismissive.

"Sorry to bother you. Holden sent me over. Is Magnolia home?"

She took a drag of her cigarette and then looked behind her. There was a smell about her that took me a moment to place. It wasn't the latest perfume from Paris. It was whiskey. I recognized it from the night Ben and I dined with Nolan Hill. It radiated from her pores. "I suppose she is." Her voice was irritated yet still painfully polite. She shouted over her shoulder. "Magnolia. Someone's here to see you."

I waited for her to invite me to come in, and when seeing that would not happen, shifted slightly on the porch.

She pushed her sunglasses down her nose, revealing a pair of bloodshot eyes. "And just who are you?"

"I'm Dot Morgan. Holden sent me over with his choice of music for the wedding."

"Oh. The wedding." She referred to it like it was a dentist appointment she had been avoiding. No wonder she hadn't shown up for the fitting. She didn't want to be a part of the wedding, which also might translate to her not wanting a new son-in-law. I tried to keep things light.

"I was there the other day when your daughter was being fitted for her wedding gown."

"I see." She inhaled from her cigarette, smoke releasing through her nose. Magnolia came rushing down the stairs.

"Dot?"

"Hello Magnolia. Holden wanted me to deliver these to you."

"Wonderful. Thanks for stopping by. I see you've met my mother, Marietta?" She looked through the list. "I like what he's picked out."

Her mother looked over her shoulder. "You can't play that song at a wedding. What will people think? I'll bet the organist hasn't even heard of it."

She was looking at "Oh, Pretty Woman." It wasn't the traditional wedding fare, but it was very romantic.

"Please, mother. We can actually play music that was written during this century, and it's for the reception, not the church service."

"I should have known that of all my daughters, my underachieving daughter would choose to marry a radio disc jockey. Iris married a doctor, and Susan married a lawyer, but no, you married someone who spins records in a broken-down radio station."

When I first saw Magnolia, she was confident and self-assured. As her mother criticized her, she shrank in stature. The confidence was replaced by a quiet resentment.

"You don't know what you're talking about, mother."

"You're the one who doesn't know." Her words slurred. "I'm not even sure your father and I will even attend your wedding."

I felt that if I didn't interrupt, they would keep on arguing. "I'm sure it's been stressful with all that's happened."

"What are you talking about, girl?" Marietta asked.

Before I could answer, Magnolia took me by the arm and pulled me further inside. "Come with me, Dot." Once we got into a front parlor area, she closed the folding doors. "If you don't mind, please mention nothing about Joyce to my mother. As you can tell, she's not for this wedding, and if she were to find out that there's any kind of scandal attached to Holden, then she would get the wedding called off. As you may have figured out, I'm not exactly the favored daughter in this house. All I want to do is get out of here and live with Holden. At least he loves me. I know parents are not supposed to have a favorite child, but my mother had two favorites, neither of which was me."

"I'm sorry. I didn't know." I also didn't know her mother was a morning drinker.

"My brother went against my mother, and my parents disinherited him. We don't even know where he lives now."

"When was the last time you heard from him?"

"Two years ago. Sometimes I feel sorry for him not being able to be here, and other times I'm jealous. My brother was, shall we say, not the marrying type."

My eyes widened as I was unsure of what she was trying to say to me.

"You know. He didn't like girls."

"Oh."

"I may dislike my family and how they've treated me, but I don't want to be disowned by them. It would break my heart and, to be honest, having no money in my future could be difficult for Holden and me. We have plans for the radio station. You can understand that, can't you?"

I certainly could understand what she was saying. If her mother disowned her, it was a way of canceling any kind of security that she and her new husband would have running the radio station. It was all about the money.

Chapter Thirteen

When Gerald came to work that afternoon, there was a spring in his step.

"You had a call today." I handed him a slip of paper with the caller's name and number. "He wanted to know about setting a time?"

Gerald took the paper and raised his chin slightly. "Thanks, Dot. I'll take care of it."

"I've never heard of this guy. Is he going to sing on the air?"

"Like I said, I'll take care of it."

"Is there something going on that I need to know about?"

Then there it was. Gerald had the most beautiful smile of any man I'd ever seen. When he flashed it, it seemed to shut down any misgivings anyone would have. "Not at all."

I remembered the sheet music I found on the floor. "Does this have something to do with the music that we found in the lobby the other day?"

"What music?" If I wasn't sure I had found the music, I could begin to doubt myself.

It was amazing how well he was putting me off. The more he evaded me, the more I knew Gerald had a secret. It had something to do with that sheet music, and it was happening on his shift. He spent most of the night alone. We all went home, except for the news and sports guy and they left after six. Gerald read any news reports they left for him. I gazed at him for a minute, judging if I'd be able to get him to confess to anything here and now. He wasn't budging. The only way I was going to find out anything was to sneak in during his shift. What would an unexpected visitor happen upon? Was

66

Gerald recording himself singing "Love Will Find a Way?" It would be pretty tough, doing that and attending to the station, but it had to be something like that.

That night, when I returned to the apartment, I found Ellie feverishly sewing a wedding dress. "Who's that one for? Is it yours?"

"No. This one is for Magnolia Daniels. I started rolling on it, and I think I'll have it done in time for her."

"Oh, she will be so happy to hear that. She's had a dramatic week. This will be something that'll help her out."

"I sure hope so. I sure wouldn't want Holden's mother for my mother-in-law."

"She did put the pressure on, didn't she?" We both laughed. She looked up from her sewing.

"And when will I be sewing one of these up for you?"

I blushed. "I don't know."

"Ah, come on, you and Ben look at each other with those big puppy dog eyes. It won't be long. You guys are having a little rough patch. It happens all the time."

"Do you think so? Lately, I'm not so sure."

"What do you mean? You crazy kids are in love. It's plain to see."

"I thought so too, but couples are supposed to decide things together. At least talk about important things, like job changes. He went through the interview at the *Dallas Morning News,* and he never even dropped a hint about it. I'm thinking I misjudged our relationship. I hate to admit it, but I caught myself having some feelings for my boss, just because he was nice to me. He's an engaged man."

Ellie tied a knot in her thread, clipped it, and then threaded another needle. "He is also very handsome, and you were feeling neglected. Ben taking the job and not telling you was a little strange, I'll admit. Did he give a reason for doing it the way he did?"

"No, nothing. I feel like an afterthought." I let out a sigh, leaned my head back, and stared at the ceiling. Was I just the girl he dated in Camden, soon to be replaced by the girl he will date in Dallas? Women in Dallas had to be a better breed than someone in a small town. They'd be more sophisticated, more worldly. Things I didn't feel very good at.

"So why don't you talk to him about it? Al and I are in premarital counseling over at the church, and the pastor says the most important thing in a marriage is communication. You're feeling angry and confused because Ben stopped communicating."

Ellie's solution sounded simple, too simple. "Just ask him?"

"Sure. That puts it on him."

"I suppose, but you just used the word 'premarital,' which we aren't even close to yet."

"And don't rush that either. If he can't explain, then maybe you're finding out something about him in the nick of time. Secrets are never good between a couple."

"I suppose you're right. You're going to think this is crazy, but I think Holden Ramsey has been flirting with me and I'm enjoying it. A year ago, I wouldn't have looked at him twice. Everything is changing, especially with Ben. If I find out he's purposely kept me away and is moving on, then I suppose I'll have to as well."

Ellie interrupted. "Oh, stop that. Ben would never hurt you that way. As far as Holden goes, I'm sure I know who started it, and it wasn't you. If, for some strange reason, you and Ben don't work out, like the world ending, then I guess you have to move on. With your looks, it won't take long if you want to date someone else. You might need a little time off to spend building confidence in yourself. It's called self-love. Isn't that crazy?"

"Yeah, crazy," I replied quietly. What I didn't tell Ellie was that someone's face flashed in my mind when she mentioned dating someone else. It was a smile, a twinkle in a set of deep blue eyes. It was not Ben. It was Holden.

Chapter Fourteen

On Friday, Ben called me at work. "Hey Dot, what are you doing tonight?"

It was as if we didn't have this deep emotional chasm between us. We hadn't spoken much since the movie, so this call was a surprise. "I don't know. What do you have in mind?"

"I thought maybe we could go on a picnic?"

"At night?"

"Come on, Dot. It's almost June, and the sun doesn't go down until after seven. We'll make it a supper picnic. What do you say? There are a few things we need to discuss."

His last few words caused my heart to register a hollow feeling. "You're right. We have a lot to talk about." The thing that bothered me the most, though, was when people leave town, they tie up loose ends, and I couldn't help but think that I was one of those things. This was it. He was going to break up with me. "Sure, what time?"

"I'll pick you up after work."

I felt closer to Ben than anyone else I had ever dated. Even though I thought of our relationship as casual, if we broke up, it would break my heart. I had to reason this out. Yes, we dated, but neither one of us professed it was serious. No one had said those three little words, "I love you." It just didn't seem necessary. I needed to prepare myself for the worst. It wasn't like I was on my way to being a lonely spinster.

I could still attract men, as was obvious in my boss's eyes. Holden's flirting was also something I couldn't stop thinking about. Maybe it was all in my mind. I liked Magnolia Daniels and sometimes, even though she was much richer than I was, I felt sorry for the girl. Her mother was hard to handle, and it made me value my own. During a slow time at work, I called my mother and told her about Ben's invitation.

"That sounds promising."

"Mom, he's about to go out of town for a new job at the *Dallas Morning News*. I think he wants to break up with me."

"Did you ever think he may be getting ready to pop the question? And why not? You two have been inseparable for quite a while now. We've all been talking about it at the library. Angie Larson started a betting pool a month ago, choosing which month Ben would propose. I have a dollar riding on June, but that's okay. This could be it!"

Had they really? Was the whole town watching and waiting for Ben and I to proclaim something more serious in our relationship? It boggled my mind. More people needed to get TVs in their homes so they would stop watching their neighbors.

"Come on, Mom. This is not that big of a deal."

"I don't think you quite grasp the situation. I think Ben is serious about you. You'd best get ready for something."

Those words kept playing over in my mind like a needle at the end of a record when Ben and I walked out to the gazebo at Camden City Park. His mother had packed a basket of fried chicken, chocolate cake, some potato salad, and carrot sticks. Once we got ourselves settled in, I broached the topic.

I picked at my potato salad. "I think you should know when you asked me to go on this picnic, people in my family got pretty strange."

Ben lay on his side facing me on the red plaid blanket, also furnished by his mother. "What do you mean?"

My heart was beating so hard, I worried he could see it through my blouse. If he wasn't going to open this conversation, I would. Sometimes, waiting on a man to do the right thing was right up there with fairytales and glass slippers. Princes almost never knocked on doors with shiny footwear. "Well, and this is going to make you laugh, but they think you are going to propose

70

to me or something. Isn't that crazy?"

Ben gulped. The voice that came out next was a squeak. "They did?"

I tried not to laugh, but I couldn't help myself. He looked like Barney Fife encountering a ghost in a haunted house.

"They sure did."

"Why would they think that?"

His question stopped everything in my heart. I guess somewhere in the back of my mind, I hoped he had been about to ask me to marry him. Couples dated for a year and then they got married. That's just how it was done. Well, that is everybody but Al and Ellie. It took them years to come around to that notion.

"You didn't believe them, did you?" He looked amazed at this new information.

An uncomfortable silence fell between us. He wasn't planning to ask me to marry him. This was just fried chicken in the park, as advertised. I felt like a fool and was fighting my instinct to flee the scene.

"No, but we have been together for a while now."

He nodded. "I guess I didn't think about that. I don't know, Dot. You and I are just comfortable together. I'm not going to deny that I think you're beautiful, and I love kissing you, but, well, things are happening for me. Is that awful?"

What he was saying wasn't that far off from my own feelings, but that he was saying it was heartbreaking. I guess deep down inside, I wanted more from him. "Sort of."

"You're disappointed."

"Why would I be disappointed? I guess I was just being silly. You're right. We've had a lot of fun together, and that's really all that matters. It's not like we're Romeo and Juliet, right?" I gave the best fake laugh I knew how. This picnic was turning into a nightmare. I just wanted to go home and crawl under the covers and die.

He laughed, too, and I wasn't sure how real it was. "Yeah. Not like Romeo and Juliet or anything. Some time apart will be good for us. Nolan says I'm right where a junior reporter should be at this stage in my career. I'm glad you're so understanding about this. This job in Dallas is important to me. It's exactly what I want to be doing next with my life. I think if I could just get in there, I could write stories worthy of a Pulitzer. Don't you?"

I tried to feign enthusiasm, but I couldn't. "Well then, as long as it's all about you, then I guess we don't have any problems." I felt anger rising in me. The heat on my neck, the weight in my chest. I couldn't help it. "I'm so sorry, but I'm suddenly not very hungry. Good luck in your new job, Mr. Dalton." I rose from the bench. My apartment was only two blocks away, and the walk would stop me from further enduring this moment of defeat. Even though it was a beautiful spring day, I felt like I was walking home in a cold, lonely blizzard. Ben was a self-serving jerk who had just left behind a war zone of damage in my heart.

As I walked, I realized I had way too much energy to go back home. I decided to check out what Gerald was up to during his shift. For a moment, I thought about taking Ben with me, which now seemed like a stupid idea. I had been making a lot of misjudgments when it came to Ben. No, I would do this one on my own. No matter what was going on, Gerald was a nice guy, and right now, I needed his friendship.

When I got to the radio station, the door was locked. Gerald always locked it at night because he was in there all by himself. I dug in my bag for the key that Holden had provided for me and quietly unlocked the door. The lights from the DJ booth streamed into the lobby, giving me enough visibility to go across and past my desk. At first, I thought that there wasn't anybody in the DJ booth, but then a young man with warm brown skin sat up after it looked like he had been retrieving something from the floor. I shrank back against the wall. Who was this guy?

He couldn't have been over seventeen or eighteen at the most. As he looked down at a record cover, I did a commando move against the wall and made my way to the hallway, out of the line of sight of the DJ booth. If Gerald was not in the booth, that meant he must be in the studio. I had tried to figure out how he could record himself singing and work on the radio, and now I had the answer. He had a young accomplice. Probably a happy one as well. What teenage boy wouldn't want to play records on the radio?

I passed the other offices, and the door to the studio, which was normally locked, was open just a crack. A beautiful piano solo of "Love Will Find a Way," a song by Sam Cooke that I'd heard Gerald play at night, drifted my way. The singer began as soft, mellow voices of several men backed him up. Suddenly, a solo voice took over, and it was one I recognized—at least, I thought I did. Was that Gerald?

No. Still, I recognized that voice. I listened some more to the soft baritone sounds.

I had heard that voice before, but it wasn't here in the studio; it was on the radio. I stepped closer to the door to get a better look in, and to my surprise, the small studio was filled with singers and a man at the piano wearing sunglasses. The voice came to me clearly now, and I realized who it was.

I was looking at Ray Charles, the famous musician. No one had seen me yet, and I spotted Gerald running the soundboard. I didn't know these microphones and stands existed back here. The most incredible aspect of everything was that Ray Charles was here recording.

Suddenly, the music stopped. I worried they had seen me and stepped back into the shadows. I should have made them aware of my presence, but I wanted just one more stolen moment.

"No. We've got to run that one more time. You were late on your entrance again," Ray said to one singer. "If you're not there on time, it messes up the whole rest of the song. Concentrate."

I noticed a few beads of sweat on top of Ray's brow. The temperature in the room was not incredibly warm, but he looked overheated. I had read in the past how Ray had trouble with drugs and had been arrested a couple of times. The man was so talented that it really was a shame that he was battling this demon. I wanted to hear him sing some more. I leaned just a little closer, and the door creaked. If the musicians had been singing, no one would have heard it, but they hadn't. All eyes turned to me, including Gerald's.

"Hello there, who is this?" Ray asked from the piano.

Gerald came running out of the sound booth. "Sorry, Ray. She works here." He came closer to me, working his way through the singers. "Dot, what are you doing here?"

"I was curious."

"I can't believe you were so nosy you had to sneak in like this. You just couldn't mind your own business, could you?"

"Is there a problem here?" Ray asked.

Gerald was nervous in all his movements and twisted around to address him. "No problem at all, Mr. Charles. She's about to leave. We won't waste any more of your time. We know we're lucky to get you here, right, gentlemen?"

I would not let this opportunity pass me by to speak to the one and only Ray Charles. "It's nice to meet you, Mr. Charles."

A smile spread across his face, and he extended his hand. I walked over. "Well," he chuckled. "It's nice to meet you."

"What's your name?"

"Dot." I put my hand in his. "I'm a fan. It's really an honor that you're here at our station. I work as the receptionist here, you know, answering the phones." I realized I was rattling on, but Ray just kept smiling.

"Yes, I can see how you'd be good at that. You have the gift of gab."

"And Dot is going home. She's seen what she came to see." I felt Gerald's hand on my waist as he guided me away from Ray Charles.

"Such an honor to meet you. Nice to meet you all," I said as Gerald pushed me out the door. He turned back to the assembled crowd.

"I'll be right back. It'll give you a chance to fix that part."

Gerald's flashy smile was replaced by a scowl. His shoulders stiffened. "All right, Dot. Let's be honest here. Are you going to get me fired?"

"Get you fired? Of course not. Just tell me what's going on. I can't believe I just met Ray Charles. You're using the recording studio. I didn't know you even knew how to do that."

Gerald looked around him as if expecting to find Holden materializing out of the woodwork like a blob from a science fiction movie on a Saturday afternoon matinee. "If I tell you this, I'm trusting you. I don't trust many people." He paused another minute and then finally spoke. "We've been using the studio at night for a while now. Joe in there is part of The Harmony

Kings, and he knew Ray Charles from some gigs he did in Kansas City. He got Ray to come and record a song, and we've got big hopes for it. Ray said he'd be glad to if Atlantic Records didn't mind it. We're waiting on that, but we're making the recording, anyway. I had to use the studio. I just had to. There is nothing in this area to record music, and it's a sideline. A sideline I'm taking money for, and that is how I could lose my job. We make the tapes here and send them off to a record company in Nashville. I never got permission from Holden, but that doesn't mean I didn't ask him. He kept putting me off, but I kept having artists come to me who wanted to record. It's tough to get into a recording studio in Dallas, especially if you're..."

"Colored?"

"The world is full of wonderful music and that doesn't mean it's being sung by Perry Como or Dean Martin. When you found "Love Will Find a Way," that was left by The Harmony Kings, who do a great version of it. We just want to get our music out on the radio, but it seems there's a big white door in the way. A door marked 'No Negros Welcome.'"

I had grown up in Camden, but really couldn't say I'd ever had a friend like Gerald. This was an experience that I had never encountered before. Gerald and his friends had to live by a completely different set of rules. I knew things were changing and that marches were going on in Washington, but this was the first time I had ever really felt Gerald's struggle. I also knew that it took a lot for him to confide in me. I wouldn't disappoint him. "You know what, if it isn't hurting anybody, then I don't see a problem in it."

The smile was back, and Gerald's shoulders relaxed. "You promise? You're not going to go running and tell Holden after this, are you?"

"Only if you want me to. The only thing I have problems with is you are using Holden's equipment and making money off this venture."

"I know." He put a hand up over his forehead. "That's the part that bothers me, too. To make it right, I saved a percentage of the money I'm making and put it in a savings account. When Holden finds out, I'm hoping to offer him that cash and it'll smooth the waters a bit."

That simple gesture proved to me that Gerald was an honest man. "Sounds like you've got it figured out. If you get any more calls during the day, I'll take your messages and give them to you when you come on shift at night. That sound good?"

"It sure does. Thank you, Dot."

"Then it's settled."

As I walked out of the radio station, I felt a tiredness wash over me. I'd spent the evening with a man whose ambition was causing him to take a job at a newspaper in Dallas without telling his girlfriend. Then I discovered a man whose ambition had him sneaking around at night making records that might not even be legal. Now I understood the walls Gerald was up against because of the color of his skin. It was the most unfair thing I'd ever seen. The music that was being created in that studio was incredible, but according to white radio stations, it might not be acceptable. I wouldn't tell Holden anything. It was the least I could do.

Chapter Fifteen

"I can't believe you talked me into coming to this," Ellie said as she got out of my car after I parked in front of the Ramsey house.

"She invited you as well as me. In fact, she made sure that I would tell you that you were invited to this." I grabbed the shower gift we were giving the happy couple.

"I know, but I just have so much going on right now. The idea of taking time out for somebody else's wedding shower feels ludicrous."

She was right. I hoped they wanted to thank her for going all out to get Magnolia's wedding dress ready, and this was their way of doing it. I hadn't been working at the radio station that long and didn't know any of Magnolia's friends, so having my cousin along would make things a lot easier for me. "Even if you're not glad you're here, I am. It wouldn't be any fun without you."

She put her hand over mine and squeezed it. "Yeah, yeah, yeah. I love you, too. Let's just get this over with."

The house was decorated with silver bunting, white roses, and a centerpiece made of bridal netting and flowers. I was surprised as I looked around that many of the guests were older. There were people Magnolia's age there, but few. Most of the ladies there might have been friends with Leah, not the bride-to-be. I searched for Magnolia's mother but didn't see her anywhere. Upon seeing us, Magnolia came gushing across the room. "You made it. Oh, I'm so happy to see you both here." She looked genuinely delighted to see us. It wasn't long before Leah also made her way over.

"Excellent. I'm so glad you're here, Ellie."

Ellie looked surprised. "Wouldn't miss it for the world."

"You were so wonderful sending that dress over to us so quickly. It's just that there's a slight alteration that we need to make, I think. Magnolia doesn't seem to be bothered by it, but I was wondering if you could just take a brief look?"

Ellie compressed her lips in an effort to hide her frustration. They had brought her here to work on the dress, and that was all. They weren't glad to see her, but glad the help had arrived. I wondered if they would post me by the phone to take calls. "Of course. Where's the dress at? I'll look at it."

Leah took Ellie off as I placed the toaster wrapped in silver paper on a table overflowing with gifts. Judging from the size of my gift and the other gifts, there was a possibility that someone else had also bought them a toaster. I hoped not, because it was all I could afford on my secretarial salary. When I turned around from the gift table, I found Holden standing there with a cup of green punch in his hand.

"Well, look who's here. I guess this event won't be a total waste after all."

I was flattered he was happy to see me, if not a little unnerved by his greeting. "I'm surprised to see you here. I thought bridal showers were only attended by women."

He handed me the cup. "If I had it my way, I wouldn't be here at all," he said. "My mother insisted I attend. According to her, I'm supposed to help carry things and stand here and smile. Lord help me. If only this punch were spiked."

I took a sip of the punch, and indeed it was not spiked. It was a sugary, sweet concoction that was a mixture of 7UP and lime sherbet. It was delicious, but if you drank too much of it, your fillings would hurt. If that wasn't enough sugar for the shower attendees, there were tiny pastel butter mints, trays of appetizers shaped like balls with toothpicks in them, and a white frosted cake with yellow roses.

There was a noise in the hallway. It sounded like one of Leah's guests had imbibed something that hadn't come out of the punch bowl. Marietta Daniels stood in the doorway, a brown mink stole hanging haphazardly off her shoulders. Her hair had been pushed up into a bouffant just above her forehead, but a few strands hung wildly about her face. Holden immediately moved to her to help her balance as she wobbled precariously on her heels.

"Mrs. Daniels, Magnolia didn't expect you," Holden said. "She'll be so happy you came."

"Yeh, well, I didn't expect you either," she spit out. The comment registered with Holden, but the look in his eyes was friendly, like she had just remarked how happy she was to have him joining the family. His reaction was not genuine, but truly an art form of deceit.

"Why don't we get you a seat on the couch, and you can have some of the delicious food my mother has had prepared for the wedding shower," he offered.

Marietta slurred her words. "What is it? Beanie Weenies? Ants on a Log? Is that what the simple folk eat and call appetizers?"

The clicking of heels came up behind us. "Mother! What are you doing here?" Magnolia's face had turned an off-white color.

"It was in the paper. I thought I'd come, even though my invitation seemed to have been lost in the mail."

"There was a reason for that," Magnolia whispered as she drew closer to her mother. "Let's go." She turned to Morris, who had been standing quietly in the corner. If Magnolia had been trying to keep Marietta's drunkenness a secret, she had failed.

"Morris, will you help me get Mother back home? I think she's taken too much of her medicine."

The ladies in the room all nodded, even with the smell of whiskey in the air.

"Sure, Miss Magnolia." Morris took Marietta's elbow and Holden went to her other side.

She turned back, wanting the last word. "Not that I wanted to be at this low-class shindig, anyway. Who knows how many of your cousins have married each other? From the looks of this crowd, it's happened at least twice."

Once Morris and Holden got Marietta out the door, the crowd settled into small groups, all talking about the scene they had just witnessed. I also heard the name Joyce Bishop a couple of times, but never directly to Leah. How many of these ladies had come to Magnolia's shower to celebrate her, and how many of them were there to gather gossip about the murder? When Holden returned twenty minutes later, Leah was trying desperately to get the party back on track with "Wedding Charades." It was surreal to watch.

"If I could pick anywhere in the world to be right now, it wouldn't be here," Holden said quietly.

I admired him for how quickly he handled the situation. "I think it's very nice that you're here. You really have to love somebody to come to a party full of women playing goofy games."

"I guess so." He looked around the room. "I can see you're fitting in just as well as I am."

After that, the shower went on as prescribed, more games and the opening of gifts. I took a second cup of punch out of boredom and found it was no longer virgin. Somebody had poured something strong into it. At one point, Leah tapped on her Timex watch. "Ladies, don't leave yet. I've called the *Camden Courier,* and they are going to be here to take all our pictures to put on the society page."

"That's wonderful," a woman with a deep voice said. "Too bad Magnolia's mother didn't stay. Having her in our picture would have been so impressive."

I sensed an immediate discomfort in the room. The woman's idle comment had sparked a nerve in our hostess, and several of the older ladies also seemed to sense it. I had a feeling, the last thing Leah Ramsey wanted was a picture of drunk Marietta on the front page. Another much older lady grumbled, "I'm not going to wait for some reporter. I'm going to need help to my car."

Leah gritted her teeth. "Can't you stay another ten minutes?"

"Nope. It's been fun, and blessings on your wedding, Magnolia, but that's enough for me."

"Very well." Leah plastered on a smile, put her hands together on her chest, and said, "Holden, help Mrs. Parker out to her car, will you?"

Mrs. Parker was about five foot two and was as wide as she was tall. She used a cane, and judging from the way she was walking, she'd made quite a few visits to the punch bowl post-spiking. She stood up and wobbled, and

Holden immediately ran to her elbow, leaning down to help her. "There you go, Mrs. Parker." As he balanced her on one side, she swayed to the other side, and I stood up and grabbed the other elbow.

"I can help."

"Thanks," he muttered. The two of us helped Mrs. Parker through the room and out to the driveway.

"That one." She pointed to a gray Ford Fairlane.

"You can't possibly let her drive home like this."

"No. I'll drive her home. I suspect this was my mother's real reason for having me stand by."

"I've been to high school dances where they didn't put that much liquor in the punch," I said.

Holden laughed, the pleasant sound filling my ears.

We helped Mrs. Parker into the back seat of her car. She only protested slightly, showing that she had better judgment on whether she should drive than whether she should drink. She leaned back and closed her eyes. As we closed her door, suddenly, Holden was at my elbow. He was much closer than he had been earlier. "Thanks for helping me. You're the best, Dot." He leaned in, and it felt like he was about to kiss me. The worst part was I was looking forward to it. I had to stop this, but the momentum of the thrill rushing through me took me down. I couldn't stop if I wanted to. He lowered his lips onto mine, and I felt a pulse between us. I wanted him to kiss me, to make up for the passion that was dimming between me and Ben. I was like a starving woman who had just been offered a banquet, and then it happened. As he kissed me, I realized the face in my head was not his or even Ben's. It was Magnolia. Glorious as this kiss was, I pulled away. Holden's fiancée sat at her shower, believing he was aiding an intoxicated, elderly woman. I couldn't do this to Magnolia. I was about to tell him he needed to stop moments like this with me or anybody else, but before I could get a word out, I saw Ben in the driveway holding his camera. He looked angry. No. He looked crushed.

I immediately turned from Holden. "Ben, it's not what it looks like."

"Really? Because it looks like to me you two are kissing in the driveway." There was anger in his voice, and I deserved every bit, but I wasn't the only one at fault. He had planned to leave town without talking to me. I was a free agent. I shouldn't even worry about this. I turned on him. "I didn't think you cared. Don't you need to go take a picture of the wedding shower?"

Without a word, he walked up the driveway. With every step, it felt like someone was taking a hammer to my heart. Why had I just let this happen? How could I let Ben go? How could I make Ben stay? I didn't have any answers, but I had just made the entire situation worse. Holden squeezed my shoulder lovingly.

Chapter Sixteen

O n Sunday afternoon, in the apartment I shared with Ellie, Mary
and I made little bags of rice for the guests to throw after Ellie and
Al's ceremony. Mary Oliva, mother of two rambunctious children,
was happy to come to our apartment and put rice into tiny net squares and
tie them up with ribbon. Ellie and Al knew many people in Camden and, by
our estimates, nearly the entire town would try to squeeze in the church and
the reception hall in the basement. Between the dresses Ellie had made for
people and the many homes Al visited regularly as an electrician, it could be
a real humdinger of a wedding. That was, of course, if Ellie had a dress to
wear. She was still cagey on the subject. If I didn't know better, it was the
last holdout on her life as a single woman.

Mary poured rice into a square. "You certainly are quiet, Dot. Everything
okay?"

I had let myself get into the repetitive motion of making the tiny bags. My
mind kept drifting back to my conversation with Ben. He hadn't called today,
and I wondered if he would call ever again. How could I have been so wrong
about us? I could have been picking out dresses this year. I had been foolish
not thinking about marriage. I was the perfect age to marry, but to do that,
you have to have a groom. "Sorry. I have a lot on my mind."

"Oh, I know. Weddings will do that. Did I tell you John's sister Isabella is
thinking about getting married again?"

"No."

"Yes, she's met a rich rancher out near Graham. Little Freddie likes him
too."

"That's good to hear." I returned to my bag-making, her words blurring into the background.

"Uh, huh. You're just overwhelmed right now. Just wait until we get the wedding over, and we'll all have a nice evening out. You and Ben can dance the night away."

I felt my eyes welling up. Ellie knew about me and Ben, but Mary did not. Would I be spending the rest of the summer explaining to people how I got dumped for a job in Dallas? If that didn't get them, I could tell them how I kissed an engaged man at his fiancée's bridal shower. "About that. Ben is busy right now with the Joyce Bishop story, so we will see less of each other. His career is very important to him."

"What? Are you kidding? That guy is bonkers over you, no matter what story he's on. He's practically one of the family."

"It seems he's been offered a job in Dallas, and he's trying to impress them with his investigative capabilities. I'm not high on his list of priorities."

"Wait a minute. A job in Dallas? You haven't told me about this. Put the rice down and look at me."

As I did what she asked, a tear escaped down my cheek.

"Oh, *Mija*. What has happened?"

"I think we're breaking up." Once the emotional door was opened, everything I had been holding back came in a gush, and Mary hugged me.

"No. That can't be true. That goofy man would give up his life for you."

I talked between gasps. "I thought he was, too, but it seems his job is the most important thing in his life right now. I thought he was going to ask me to marry him, but he acted like his leaving was no big deal. Like we never loved each other. He announced he was moving to Dallas with Al and Ellie sitting there. He never talked to me or anything. I guess I'm not as important to him as I thought."

Mary nodded her head from side to side in disgust. "Men. They think they get to make all the decisions. And this Joyce Bishop story is just that. A story. It isn't the key to anyone's future."

"It means an awful lot to Holden and Magnolia. They're afraid they'll have trouble getting married with all the negative press and gossip around town.

I'm sure she's devastated to find out her fiancé is being accused of pushing his first wife off a cliff in the past. The Colorado police ruled it an accident."

"Magnolia Daniels. Now, there's a story. Did you know she ran away several times when she was a teenager? According to the police files, she felt unloved by her own family. She also had a couple of boyfriends that weren't good for her. She's not all sweetness and light. She's a troubled young lady. I think the two of them are perfect for each other."

"My goodness. I didn't know. Poor Holden."

"Poor Holden? I can't believe you just said that. You know there is a chance that he really pushed his wife off that cliff, right?"

"I don't think so." I picked up a piece of netting. I thought about the kiss. It might have upset Ben, but it was one of those glorious curl-your-toes-and-arch-your-back kisses. How could a murderer do something like that?

"Wait, a minute." Mary looked at me curiously. "You're defending him?"

"He's innocent. A man like that could never kill his wife. Holden has a good heart."

"You have a crush on Holden Ramsey, don't you?"

Sometimes, I wish Mary did not have such good intuition about things. If the Camden Police Department ever realized this skill and used it, they would find out their file clerk was a darn good detective. "Don't be silly. He's engaged. Besides, I thought I had Ben."

"Right. Ben, who is halfway to Dallas."

Why was it when she looked straight at me and said the words, I didn't believe she trusted what I was saying?

The phone rang, and when I answered, my mother was on the other end.

"I hope I'm not interrupting anything?" She asked.

"No. Mary and I were just putting together rice bags for the wedding."

"Good. I was wondering if I could ask you to hear another revision?"

Oh boy. This book-writing thing was getting to be a little annoying. "Um, sure. Fire away."

"Thank you so much. I don't know anyone else I trust enough to read this to out loud. I wanted to add just a little more treachery to the scene, you

85

know? Here it is."

Felicia walked into the barn, and there she saw the burly soldier's shoulders of Jacob as he hefted the hay into the hayloft with a pitchfork that looked to have blood at the tips of the prongs. He turned to look at her, a darkness smoldering deep in his eyes. She caught her breath as her bosom heaved upward. He was her everything.

"Uh, yes, it certainly has treachery in it now. What's with the blood on the pitchfork? I don't really see that as very romantic, Mom."

"Is it too much?"

Mary spilled her rice. "Whose blood is on the pitchfork?"

My mom paused and then said, "Hmmm. Yes, I can see that. It's just I felt it needed a change. I'll keep working on it. Thanks, Dot."

As I hung up the phone, Mary looked like her interest was piqued. She scooped up the spilled rice. "Are you going to tell me about the blood on the pitchfork, or were you planning to keep this from the police?"

I laughed. "There is no pitchfork or blood, except in my mother's mind. She's writing a romance."

Mary raised her eyebrows. "A romance with blood in it? It sounds more like a crime scene than a romance."

"Who knows? Parents." I sighed.

"Yeah, tell me about it. I think John is about to move his mother in on me. She needs someone to take care of her. I love having her around, most of the time. I've never actually lived with her."

"Wow. Where will you put her?"

"The kids will have to room together until we can find a bigger house. I'm sure that is a fight waiting to happen."

"Can you say no?" I asked.

"I can, but I don't want to. This is John's mother and if she needs help, then it is family who will take care of her."

"No matter how difficult."

"That's about it."

Chapter Seventeen

That evening, while I washed my face and looked into the bathroom mirror, I could hear Ellie in the next room opening and closing cardboard boxes as she packed for her move into Al's home. She hadn't even noticed how quiet I had been after Mary left. But, seeing what was going on in her life, I forgave her. My thoughts continued to run like tape on a reel. First there was Ben's announcement that he was moving and leaving me behind, then I couldn't forget the look on his face when he caught me kissing another man. He was giving me the final heave-ho. Maybe I should have let the relationship get more intimate. If we had made love, maybe he wouldn't want to leave me. I didn't know how to even go from a few kisses to what happened when the screen went black in the movies, but I should by now.

I stared at myself in the mirror. I was still young. If Ben wasn't going to work out, would someone else marry me?

"You okay, Dot?"

Ellie was standing there watching me look at myself. "Oh, yes. Tired, I guess." Taking a deep breath, I asked the question. "Did you decide about the trip to Las Vegas?"

"Not yet. I could see how upset it made all of you, so I thought I at least needed to think about it. You know I've been making my own decisions for my entire life, but I'm about to marry Al, and we'll be making decisions together. That's going to take some getting used to. I need to learn how to compromise."

That was the wisest thing my cousin had ever said to me. Ellie Monroe, learning to compromise. Would miracles never cease? Just more proof Al had been incredibly good for her. I was also reminded that her sleeping with Al had put them on the road to matrimony. It was as if the answer to my troubles with Ben had been there for me to pick up all along, like walking by a shiny penny sparkling up at me on the street.

"I like the way you're thinking, Ellie. I know this is rough, but you can get through it."

"I suppose I can, but what kind of insane person am I to witness bridal meltdowns for a decade and then think that I could sail through it with no problems? Sometimes I dream about going to the justice of the peace and getting this whole wedding thing over at the courthouse. After that, we could all go out for ice cream. What do you say about that? It will be our reception."

"I say I would rather see you get married in a beautiful ceremony with all the trappings. Ice cream can be for another time. I want it to be like the pictures in all those bridal magazines."

"I know, you're right, even though I think all that nonsense in those magazines is trouble for anyone trying to get married. It seems like all the planning is going along beautifully, and then one thing throws it out of kilter. That's when I throw up my hands and want to drive off and get a quickie marriage."

"Quickie marriages are often followed by quickie divorces."

Ellie raised her eyebrows and grinned. "I've heard that."

I yawned and shifted, trying to get a kink out of my neck. I was storing tension like a squirrel storing nuts. "Long day. I think I'll turn in early."

"You and Mary must have knocked out a lot of rice bags."

"We did, but we talked too. I told her about Ben."

"What did she say?"

"That he's in love with me. It's just that I can't get over how he planned this new job in Dallas and didn't include me in the decision. It felt like he had been taking me for granted. He was acting like good old Dot will understand."

"Oh, you mean like how Al treated me for years?"

"Something like that. I also thought, and you're going to think I'm being silly, but I thought he was going to propose." I wanted to hide my face. It sounded so desperate when I said it.

"Oh, baby. I'm so sorry." Ellie drew me in and hugged me, and the tears flowed as they had with Mary. "I never liked him, anyway." Ellie patted my back.

"Yes, you did." I reminded her.

"Yes, right up to the part where he broke your heart."

"Now he's going off to the city, and he'll meet other girls. I should have let him…"

"Stop that. You don't do anything you're not dying to do, hear me? Whether you sleep with him shouldn't be the deciding factor of him marrying you. Let him run off to Dallas and become a city-it."

I loved Ellie's word for people who lived in the city. A mixture of city and idiot. The phone rang in the kitchen, and I walked over in sock feet to answer it.

"Hey Dot. I'm glad I caught you." It was Ben.

"I thought we were finished talking."

There was a pause at the other end. "It's just I've learned a few more things about the Joyce Bishop case and have just finished writing it up. I know the article might be a problem for your boss, but I just have to run with this, you understand. This is a big story, and I think it will be a great piece to impress the guys in Dallas. I know we didn't end on good terms, but I just wanted to give you fair warning that I'm still digging. I'll be in Dallas tomorrow, looking for a place, but once we get a little fact-checking, it will be in the paper." With that, he hung up the phone. When had it become so important for Ben to impress anyone? It felt like I didn't know him anymore, but I had to admit, I was happy to hear his voice at the other end. I was pathetic.

Chapter Eighteen

On Monday morning, I stacked the weekend edition of the *Camden Courier* along with Monday's paper. The feature story was an in-depth investigation of Holden Ramsey's first marriage and all the suspicions Joyce had spouted in the office. Ben had published it. The thing that made me even more angry was some of the information came directly from me. I never gave him permission to include this in the article, but it didn't matter, because he had used it. Mary had warned me repeatedly not to say anything in front of him because, even if he was handsome and very desirable, he was still a reporter, a man whose job it was to get the scoop. As I looked at the picture of Holden and his first wife on their wedding day, he had certainly gotten the scoop.

Normally, I would put the newspaper in the DJ booth next to Holden's microphone so that he could discuss the stories of the day. If I didn't put it there, he would surely notice it, so I turned the newspaper to the sports page, hoping that he would start with the scores. I was folding back the paper when Gerald came out.

"Did you get your message?" I was referring to a call he had about an appointment time.

Gerald spoke rapidly. "Yeah. Sure. Thanks."

"Who was that?"

"Oh, you know. Just a guy. He does some local music here and is trying to get the down-low on how to get a record on the radio."

I remembered what Magnolia had said about Gerald's off-the-job activities. "Magnolia said you do a lot of work with local bands, even to the point of introducing them some nights at the clubs around here. Is that true?"

Gerald took his thumb and forefinger and stroked his chin. "Man's gotta eat."

"I guess so. Maybe I'll come by and see some of these groups."

"Always appreciate a supporter."

I walked into the DJ booth and carefully laid the paper down.

"Oh yes, and our lovely station assistant, Dot, has just brought me today's news. Let's see what's brewing in the town of Camden today." He picked up the paper and shooting me a look, took the edge of the paper and folded it so that the front page was facing him. As his eyes focused on the picture, he turned pale. Dead air fell as he stared. Finally, he muttered, a voice not at all usual for him. "And now we go to a commercial."

He turned off the microphone and held up the article. "What the hell? How did this get in the paper? This is terrible. What if Magnolia's folks see this?"

"I know. I was hoping you'd find it when you were off air."

He pointed to the byline. "Ben Dalton."

"Yes," I whispered, feeling guilty for what was happening to Holden. It was my fault that Ben had just printed Holden's confidential business in the newspaper. It was especially bad because I had promised Leah I could be trusted to keep their private affairs private. Poor Holden was having his entire life poured out on the front page of the *Camden Courier*. In the past year, we'd had other things happen, but I had always trusted Ben to protect the people involved. Mary had warned me not to say too much to him. Even my mother told me to always remember that Ben was a reporter. I discounted everything they said because I guess love really is blind.

Holden looked shattered. "I can't believe they would print this. The way this sounds, it just happened. My poor mother. She'll be mortified it's on the front page for everyone to see."

"I know," I said. "I'm so sorry Ben put this in the paper."

Holden was about to say more and then suddenly looked up at me, his gaze now sharp. "Ben?" He looked down at the paper and pointed to Ben's byline. "You mean you know this Dalton guy?"

"Yes. He's my boyfriend, or at least he was."

"Your boyfriend? All this time, your boyfriend has been snooping around this story, and you had something to do with this?"

"No. I never would have let this story get into the paper."

"Then how did he find out?"

"I told him about it." My voice broke on the last word. Holden looked like I had just landed him for a sucker punch.

"How could you do that to me, Dot?"

From his hurt expression, I feared I was about to lose another job. I had been disloyal to my boss, who was just trying to work his way through an unpleasant situation. A tear slid down my cheek. I had to make him understand I would never set out to hurt him.

"I'm so sorry for this. I really didn't know. Ben is trying for a new job, and, well, I guess he thought your story was too good to pass up."

Holden closed his eyes for a second and then ran his hand through his hair, causing a single strand to fall onto his forehead. "I'm sorry too, Dot. I really am. I'm ashamed that you had to learn this about me, no matter how untrue it may be. Well, I guess we never really know people, do we? You know, when you told me you had been involved in a murder investigation in your last job, I should have seen that as an omen. Has he ever done anything like this before? Did this happen then?"

"No, never. I used to think I could trust him. Things with him are changing. He's changing."

Holden's voice became tender. "Like how?"

I felt a rush of emotion come over me. "He's had a job offer in Dallas, and I think he's going to take it. He really wants to be a crime reporter, and this is his big break. I now think he learned of your story and thought this would be what would grease the wheels. I guess he's more ambitious than I thought he was."

"Great. The guy thinks he's Walter Cronkite. I hate to have to tell you this, but I need you to keep your distance from him. If I catch you talking to Ben, then I'm going to have to let you go. There are so many people's futures on the line, and he's making the situation much worse. I'm surprised my mother hasn't called. She's going to blow up with this. Then, of course, there's Magnolia and her family. This may cancel the entire wedding."

He reached out, and it took me a second to realize he wanted to hug me. I came closer, and as he held me, it gave me assurance that I hadn't screwed everything up.

The phone rang, and I reached over Holden to answer it, but realized the closeness of our bodies. He was such a nice guy, and I felt terrible that Ben had just done this to him. I also couldn't deny I felt a little thrill being that close to him. Holden released me and returned to the DJ board.

"KDUD."

"This is Pastor Rob Roy. Is this the young lady I spoke to the other day?"

"It is."

"Heaven be praised. Could you come by today sometime? I just read the newspaper, and I'd like to talk to you again."

"Sure. I could stop by today at my lunchtime."

When I hung up, Holden had the earphones on. This was when I could have told him it was the pastor, but if I did, he'd know I went to see him the first time.

"Request?" he asked.

"No. I need to stop by my mother's library later today. No big deal." I was amazed, after that heartfelt hug, just how quickly the lie came to me.

When I returned to the pastor's office, he seemed different. Gone was the glib spokesman. Now, he seemed almost repentant.

"Thank you for making time for me today." He motioned for me to sit in a brown leather chair with slender wooden legs.

"I have to admit, I was surprised you called."

He nodded quietly. "It was after I read the newspaper that I knew I had gone too far in protecting Joyce. I now feel if I had been a little more transparent, there is a possibility she would be alive today. Please understand that I take any kind of confidential information seriously and want to protect the person who shares it with me. Also, and I'm not proud of this, I didn't take Joyce's story as wholly true."

Even though I still resented his statement about women and their tendencies toward hysteria, I reflected on the morning she came into the radio station. I thought she was a raving lunatic, and it was obvious so had he. As a pastor, Rob Roy was supposed to be listening and not judging. At least that was what they said over the door, right? Judge not, lest ye be judged?

"Well then, I guess I appreciate you calling me back to tell me the entire story, not just the one clouded by your opinion of women in general. So, what did she tell you?"

Rob Roy stood and walked over to his bookshelf as if he were about to take out a reference volume to use in an upcoming sermon. Instead, he stuck both hands in the pockets of his tan Sansabelt pants. "I know I told you her feelings about the death of his first wife, but it was more than that. It incensed her. So much so, I worried it would get her in trouble."

I wished I'd called Mary first. She could have used information like this, and I wasn't so sure he would feel comfortable sharing this in a police station. If word got around that he was violating a parishioner's trust, it could put him out of business, and from the looks of the attendance at Living Word, business was good.

"I don't think I know any more than you do, but there was one part that astounded me. She said that as Holden told her about the accident, he got excited. He was telling it like it was a ghost story around the campfire. He even smiled in parts."

"He did?" I couldn't imagine him sharing the story of his first wife's death with a smile. It was creepy to start, and it didn't do much to prove his innocence.

"Yes, and that was what scared Joyce so much. His entire attitude toward his wife's grisly death was shocking. And one other thing. He said his wife was terrified of heights. He had a tough time getting her up to that altitude. My question here is, why would a woman afraid of heights stand so close to the edge of a mountain?"

Holden had told me just the opposite. He said she liked the outdoors. He never let on a fear of heights. I sat quietly, processing Pastor Rob Roy's words.

"I know he's your boss, miss, but you are a sweet young girl. Something you might not know about Holden Ramsey is that he is considered a bit of a womanizer in Camden. Magnolia Daniels is just the first one to have hooked him, but there have been plenty of girls who have tried."

"I don't believe that."

"You should. He hasn't flirted with you, has he?"

I put a hand to my throat and felt the heat rising in my cheeks. "No. Of course not. Our relationship is purely professional, nothing more." I wondered if they sent you to hell for lying to a minister.

"Take heed, child. It's a common tale of an older, handsome man to take advantage of a young woman like you."

"I'll be careful," I muttered.

"I only say this because I feel I missed my chance to protect Joyce. Let my words and prayers be protection for you."

Chapter Nineteen

The next day, as I sat at work answering the early morning request calls, Gerald pulled up a chair next to my desk.

"It sure is getting hot, isn't it? Won't be long before the temperature stays in the nineties."

Usually, he would tell me to have a wonderful day and make a beeline for the door, so his effort and conversation this morning were puzzling. My mind was still on the pastor's words, so I barely heard him. Tracy had been afraid of heights, and Holden conveniently forgot to tell me about that part. What else was he holding back?

"Uh, huh."

"And I heard on the radio we're expecting flurries."

"Uh, huh."

"Well then, I'm glad you agree, although I'm pretty sure you do not know what I just said. What's on your mind today?"

"What do you mean?"

Gerald looked at me sideways. "Don't kid a kidder, Dot. There's something going on with you today. Does it have to do with Holden and the article that came out in the paper?"

I didn't feel comfortable revealing what was shared with me by a pastor. "Yes. That's it. It's all just so upsetting."

"My mother would say you are one of the sweet ones. You don't need to be wasting your time worrying about Holden Ramsey and the women in his life. Besides, you don't know as much about Joyce and her family as you think you do."

"What do you mean?"

Before Gerald could answer, a call came in on the request line. I checked the clock. I hadn't had my obnoxious caller from KOOL yet and hoped this wouldn't be it.

The voice on the other side was low and reminded me of the man who had left a message for Gerald. "Yeah, I was wondering if you could play "Under the Boardwalk,", but I want it to be by The Harmony Kings. Do you have that record?"

I knew we had "Under the Boardwalk," but I had never heard of the record the caller was asking about. Obviously, this was a friend of theirs trying to get played on the radio.

"What do they want?" Gerald whispered behind me.

"They want to hear 'Under the Boardwalk' by The Harmony Kings."

"I got you covered."

To my surprise, Gerald pulled a record encased in a paper sleeve out of his small leather briefcase. He gave me a big smile. A smile I wasn't sure I trusted. "Just happened to have that one. It's hot off the presses. I'm surprised there's a request for it already, but I've heard this myself, and it's a good one. If you like, I'll cover the phone, and you can take this one to Holden."

I took the record from him. What had just happened? The phone call, the convenient new purchase of a record, Gerald's chattiness. I had been set up. The small talk he had been making now made sense. He was waiting for this call to come in so that he could offer the record. I assured the caller that we would play their selection and hung up. I gave Gerald a sideways look. "You knew they were going to call, didn't you?"

Gerald feigned innocence, but his smile gave him away. "Why, Dot Morgan? I do not know what you're talking about. Sometimes luck is just with you."

I carried the record into the DJ booth, where Holden was busy forecasting the weather. "Gerald would like you to play this." When I placed the record in front of him, he raised his eyebrows, but then, accepting the LP, went back to work.

When I came back, Gerald was on the phone with another caller. A grimace came over his features. Finally, he said, "You wouldn't know good music if it hit you in the face. Don't shut the door on R&B until you've heard it, and for your information, unlike you, our music is for people of all colors. You have a great day, and keep your dial tuned to KDUD, not that loser station KOOL." He slammed the phone down.

"Another prank call from the DJ at KOOL?"

"Yes, it was." His tone was quiet yet determined. "When he got me instead of you, he recognized my voice as the night DJ. He made a few comments about the music I play being for the...I can't say it. I won't give him the pleasure of repeating it."

"Oh, Gerald. I'm so sorry."

"Don't be. It's not like this type of thing doesn't happen every day."

"Well, you certainly had the last word on it, didn't you?"

A smile crept in on Gerald's face. "I did, didn't I?"

"Yes, you did, and the best part is, he had you on the air. I wish I could come back like that on that guy."

"The thing is, his listeners love it."

"Says a lot about them as well."

As he finished speaking, Holden came over the speaker. "And now a special request from our night DJ, Jammin' Gerald. This is 'Under the Boardwalk' by The Harmony Kings. It's a little different from what we usually play, but don't go away. I have a lineup of Perry Como, Frank Sinatra, and Jerry Vale coming up for your listening pleasure."

Gerald shrugged. "He just couldn't give The Harmony Kings all the airtime, now, could he? He had to back it up with all the old white men from the fifties."

"Nope. I'm amazed he even played it."

Chapter Twenty

L ater, after Gerald had left, Holden came out of the DJ booth. "Just what was that business with that record?"

Telling on Gerald would not be good for coworker relations, so I decided that, for now, I would keep what I knew about him to myself.

I tried to look surprised. "Yes. Wasn't that strange? He was sitting here talking to me, and then we get the call, and boom, there he is with the record for you to play."

"So, what you're saying is it was a setup all along, wasn't it? People are desperate to get their records on the radio, even going so far as to give Gerald, the night DJ, a free record. I just hope they didn't pay him any money to play it. There is such a thing called payola, you know. According to Congress, this is now a misdemeanor."

"Really? They'll pay a DJ to play a record?"

"Oh yes. I'm surprised you haven't heard about that. Big stink, but this is a local band, so I don't know how much it could hurt. It's not like people in Dallas are listening to our station." Truth be told, there weren't that many people listening in Camden, either.

I supposed he was right. It was harmless, but just a little surprising about Gerald that he would do something like this. As Holden turned to head back to the DJ booth, the phone rang.

I nodded and answered the phone. "KDUD."

"Good." It was Mary, and she sounded excited. "I got you on the phone. Do you think you could come down to the station at about 12:05?"

"I guess so. Why?"

"I'll tell you when you get here."

As I hung up the phone, Holden stood with a finger to his chin, watching me. "Now, that didn't seem like a record request."

"It wasn't. My friend Mary wants me to meet her at the police station."

"Was she arrested? I'm amazed. For someone who looks like a Saturday matinee sweetheart, you keep finding yourself in the middle of trouble."

"It's nothing like that. Mary is a cop."

Holden's shoulders straightened. "Even more unexpected."

When I entered the police station, Mary sat alone at her desk that faced the front lobby counter. Officer Jerry, the man who usually stood at the counter working with people and their various complaints, had already left for lunch. This was a routine that Mary and I had established quite some time ago. Whenever Officer Jerry was in the room, we had to watch what we said. It was best to visit when he took his lunch. Mary was on the phone.

"Yes, Mama. We keep the towels there. It seemed like a good spot to me. Yes, well, move them if you like."

She rolled her eyes and hung up the phone. "Abuela has moved in. God help me. I sent up a prayer to St. Jude. Still waiting on that one."

From being around Mary, I had learned St. Jude was the saint of impossible causes. Her mother-in-law situation must have been really bad. "Hopefully, it will get better. What's going on?"

"Come and look. We found wife number one's diary at the pet shop."

"Don't you mean Joyce's diary?"

"Nope. She had the diary of Holden's first wife. And after reading it, it's no surprise she got herself killed." She handed me a small green leather journal.

"How did Joyce get her hands on this?"

Mary shrugged. "I'm really not sure, but I know she visited Tracy's family. It was in the police report she had made when she accused Holden of murdering her. All I can guess is they gave it to her, or she took it when nobody was looking."

When I opened it, the neat handwriting filled the pages with an entry for almost every day. As I read through a few pages, Holden's wife, Tracy, seemed to be a sweet person. She wrote about how wonderful it was to be married to him. I closed the journal. "Really, Mary. I feel like the intimacy of a new bride is none of my business."

Mary took the small book from me and leafed to another entry. "Read this part. It's about a month before she died."

The handwriting that had been so orderly and concise in the first half of the diary now looked erratic, even scribbled in some parts.

"What I thought had been a figment of my imagination was not. It's getting worse and worse. I don't know what to do. I don't know who to talk to about this. It may sound silly, but as much as I love Holden, I no longer feel safe around him."

I looked up to see Mary watching me read. She took the diary from me and paged through it to another page. "Read this part."

July 9th, 1962.

Holden thinks going out of town will be good for me, but I am not so sure. I'm still terrified, and I feel like I don't have anyone to speak with. Every time I try to call my mother, the phone line clicks dead. I can't explain it, but right now, I feel so alone."

My gaze returned to Mary. "See what I mean? She was in danger. Joyce was in danger, too. We should have listened to her."

"Yes." Mary shifted slightly and drew in a breath. "Yes, she was innocent, but that doesn't mean that the Bishop family hasn't been in the hallowed halls of the police station."

"What are you saying? Don't tell me Joyce had a police record."

"Not Joyce. It's her father. He was a real character."

Gerald's words came back to me about his father being falsely accused. "Actually, I knew about that."

"Yeah. He got a guy put in jail once. These Bishops, once they get a cause, they just don't stop until something happens."

I thought about Gerald's story. They arranged for a form of justice, even though it was based on a lie. Had Joyce tried to make things right for Tracy because of what she had seen growing up with her father? This diary and the fact that Joyce was dead were serving as a lesson to me. Thinking about what had happened to Joyce confirmed in me that sometimes trying to find out more can put you in peril yourself. I would have to be more careful.

Chapter Twenty-One

That night, when I got home from work, I had Joyce's diary on my mind. When Ellie came up behind me in a wedding veil, I didn't even know she was there. "Oh! I didn't see you. I thought you were a ghost in all that white." It was reassuring she was finally wearing something that might lead to the mysterious wedding dress she had yet to start, but that was just the problem. Where was the rest of the outfit? "Is that your veil?"

Ellie did a twirl, her hands at the front of the veil. "Yes. Do you like it?"

"I love it." There were little white flowers appliqued onto the veil that crowned my cousin's head. Her fine handiwork made a simple piece of tulle look like an heirloom.

"Do you have the dress, too?" I asked, a little hope glimmering in my voice.

Ellie yanked off the veil. "Nope. Not today."

"Will I see it before the wedding?"

"Who knows? Maybe I'll have a nudist wedding."

"I certainly hope not."

"Just kidding. I plan to wear clothes. There are some people in this town I don't want to see in the all-together."

"Glad you feel that way."

"So, you and Ben? Are you going to be all right for the wedding? You're not going to have some sort of a shouting match or anything, right?"

The wedding. Ben. I had purposely put that entire issue on the shelf, trying not to think about it. I felt overcome with emotion. My words running together, I told Ellie about the kiss I shared with Holden at the shower. "I messed it all up. I never ever should have let him kiss me," I said at the end of my confession, my former tears now replaced with self-loathing.

"Are you sure that Ben saw? I mean, maybe you could say he thought he saw something, but he didn't actually see something. Put it all back on him."

Even though Ellie's idea was inventive, Ben was a reporter, and he knew what he saw. Plus, it seemed really mean. I was mad at Ben, but I didn't want to make him doubt himself in this. "I guess I've proven this year that I can't keep a job, and now I can't keep a man."

Ellie patted my shoulder to comfort me. "Now. It isn't all that bad. You can get him back."

"There's no way we can stay together at this point."

Ellie didn't immediately respond. "If that's the way you feel. I have to think you'll be dating somebody after Ben, right? I mean? Is he your one?"

Was he? "I don't know."

Ellie slapped her leg as an idea hit her. "That's it. We're going out."

"Going out? Where are we going?"

"We're going out for a drink."

Now, Ellie and I considered ourselves women of the world, but even though she was in her thirties and I was in my twenties, we'd never really actually gone out for drinks. I know it sounds frightfully old-fashioned, but we just never had. I wasn't even sure how to go out for drinks.

"Where will we go?"

"We're heading to the Uphill." The Uphill Bar was aptly named because there were two bars in Camden. One in town and one up the hill. The one in town was for the regular drinkers, but the Uphill catered more to people meeting people who didn't want their cars seen by people at the Western Auto which was situated right next to the local watering hole. That kind of thing.

"Not Finley's?"

"No. Finley's has too many drunks in it. Besides, word would get back to our mothers we were out drinking on a weeknight. We're heading to the Uphill."

Ten minutes later, I was straightening the hem of my skirt as we sat at the bar. Ellie ordered me a rum and coke. She ordered a beer for herself. I gaped at her as she deftly took a swig.

"What? I drink beer with Al all the time."

I had sipped a few sips of my drink, but frankly, the rum was ruining the taste of the Coke.

"I've never seen you drink beer."

"There are a lot of things you have never seen me do, but that doesn't mean I have been doing them." Ellie winked. The band that evening was The Harmony Kings. I leaned over and told Ellie about Gerald bringing in the record to the business and how it made Holden suspicious.

Ellie took a sip of beer. "That was convenient. I wonder what's going on there."

Before I could answer, the band went on break, and the leader came over to get drinks, squeezing in right next to me. After ordering, he turned to me and grinned. "I know you. You work with my friend Gerald. Don't you?"

"I do. I think we played your record on the air today."

The man gave me an enormous smile and extended his hand to shake mine. "And for that, I thank you. My name's Joe Nichols, and what's yours?"

"Dot Morgan."

"Well now, Dot Morgan, any friend of Gerald's is a friend of ours. Everyone on The Harmony Kings wants to thank you for playing our record today."

"Oh no. I didn't play your record. My boss did."

His drinks were presented in front of him, and he grabbed one of the amber liquid, took a drink, and then gave me that dashing smile again. "Sure, your boss did. But he never would have done it if you hadn't handed it to him. It seems when people who look like me hand that man a record, he won't play it. No, we needed a young, beautiful maiden such as yourself."

Was Holden so bigoted that he refused to play music by bands that weren't white and singing songs from ten years ago? It couldn't be right. "I think you're just being nice."

"Yeah, probably. Being nice can be a luxury, and people have to choose to do it. Gerald chose to do it for us. He has not had an easy road of it, you know." Joe held up the drinks, and members of the band came off the stage. They gathered around us.

The singer, a beautiful woman in a red satin dress, smiled and tapped on Joe's shoulder. "You got yourself a girlfriend already?"

"Better than that. This is the lady who handed our record over to be played on KDUD today. More of the band came up behind her. "I was just telling her about what happened to Gerald's family."

There was some hemming and hawing, and then the singer spoke up. "I'm Val. It was a terrible thing. Just another case of an innocent man going to jail, but nobody seems to care about that. Not if he comes from our side of the tracks."

Ellie edged forward. She took a drink of her beer and then blurted, "What happened? I'm dying to know now."

The singer leaned her head closer to her. "Pretty simple. A good old boy crashes his car, lies about it, and the judge locks up one of us. It was Gerald's daddy who got blamed, and he had nothing to do with it. He ended up going to prison for years. Later, they found out they had made a mistake, but they did nothing to pay back Gerald's daddy. The Bishops to this day claim they are victims and have never ever apologized to Gerald's family."

Ellie scowled. "Couldn't they appeal it?"

"And take the chance that the next white judge gives him more time?"

"That's not right."

Val grabbed a glass filled with water and a slice of lemon off the bar and took a drink. "That's how things work, you know."

As I sipped on my rum and coke, I decided I was starting to like the taste of it. What I didn't like was the story I was being told about what had happened to Gerald's family. How could something so unfair happen to a man just because the color of his skin differed from the judge's? I thought about how that would have made me feel if my father had been placed in jail for something that he didn't do. Maybe it was the rum firing me up, but I had just been awakened to the fact that people were not always treated fairly. What I really wondered was how angry had it made Gerald? Had he been angry enough to kill Joyce to get back at the Bishop family? I thought back of all the times I had ever spent with Gerald at work. He did not seem to be a violent man. He was just the opposite. I couldn't believe Gerald would ever do anything as awful as murder, but he probably thought no one would ever do something like wrongly accuse his father and put him in prison. It was something to think about.

This man's words put a tilt into my world. Three years of your life gone, just on someone else's say-so. I barely noticed when another band member extended his hand, gesturing for me to dance to music playing on the jukebox. I rose and joined him on the floor, all the while thinking of how unfair it was and, worse, how it was going on in this idyllic little town I'd thought was perfect.

We danced to a slow ballad, and he twirled me. "I'm sorry. I don't even know your name."

"Jasper, and you're Dot."

We smiled and continued our dance. Jasper was nice, tall, and built like a football player, and up on stage, he played keyboards. When he laughed, there was a low rumble in his chest.

I was enjoying the dance when someone tapped Jasper's shoulder.

"Excuse me, I think you're dancing with my girl."

Ben stood before us, and his cheeks were burning with anger. How did he even know where Ellie and I were? Where had he come from, and was he seriously going to insult this man on the dance floor?

"I'm sorry, I didn't realize." Jasper stepped back.

"You don't have to do that," I said to Jasper.

"Somehow, I think I do." Jasper gave Ben a nod and handed me to him.

"Thanks." Ben took me by the waist, and we danced away. It was not the peaceful, easy dance I had shared with Jasper, but there was a feeling of combustion between us.

"What do you think you're doing?" Ben asked.

"What do you mean, and why do I need your permission? We broke up, remember? Ellie brought me here because I was upset."

"By what?"

"By you, what else would it be?"

Ben bit his lower lip and tightened his grip on my waist. "I'm sorry for that. If you must know, I've never really had a girlfriend like you before. I know I probably handled this whole thing wrong, and I've hurt you, but to come to a place like this and dance with—"

"A colored man?"

"No. I didn't mean it like that. It's just we hear things about this place at the paper all the time. When Al called and told me Ellie came out here with you, I started worrying for your safety."

That explained a lot of things.

We continued dancing. "I can take care of myself. The biggest danger I've been in lately is from ambitious reporters stomping on my heart. Your plans to leave hurt me, you know?"

"I know. We were having such a fun time, I didn't think about it. You're comfortable, Dot, like a magnificent pair of shoes."

"Great, it's not true love; it's loafers to you!"

"Come on, it's not like that, and you know it."

"It's just that Ellie's getting married, my boss is getting married…"

Ben scowled. "Holden getting married. Please. What was he doing kissing you with his bride-to-be inside?"

"I don't know, but I stopped him as soon as it happened."

He nodded as if he were beginning to believe me. That day, he wasn't ready to listen, so caught up in his own anger. Today, he took it in quietly.

"Okay. What about this guy you're dancing with?"

My neck stiffened. "He's a friend of Gerald's from the office. He asked me to dance, and I said yes. You know, for a guy who doesn't think of himself as attached to me, you sure think I'm attached to you."

He drew me closer. "Aren't you?"

He kissed me. Even though the song had switched from ballad to jitterbug, we stood still, lost in our own world. Our kisses were like Burt Lancaster and Deborah Kerr's in *From Here to Eternity*, surrounded by a sea of people.

I had never felt like this.

When we finally stopped kissing, I was out of breath.

"I knew it. I knew you loved me," Ben said as he pulled me closer. The rest of the dancers were doing the pulls and pushes of the jitterbug, but Ben and I stayed together, my hand in his, resting on his chest. "A woman who kisses like that is in love."

"Idiot. Yes, I love you. If I didn't, I wouldn't have reacted the way I did. I loved you, and maybe I didn't even realize it. We got too comfortable together. I guess I took you for granted."

Ben spun me around, and then we returned, our bodies close to each other. "Yes, I think you're right about that."

"But then you tell me you're moving. How am I supposed to react to that? Thank God you've come to your senses." After a kiss like that, Ben would be staying in town. That wasn't a Saturday night peck on the cheek by the front door kind of kiss. That was passion. That was like Rhett and Scarlet, and I was kissed the way a woman should be kissed.

"I thought you knew how much I care for you, Dot."

His words were sincere, but one of them was wrong. I told him I loved him, and he followed it with how he cares for me. Not the same. "I thought I was a little more than that to you."

Ben stopped dancing and, taking my hand, led me off the floor, through the crowd, and into the cool evening air. Once outside, he set his thumb on my chin.

"Dot, you mean the world to me. You know that, right? But our kiss doesn't change anything. I'm still going to Dallas."

"Ben, how can you say that?"

"How can I not? Dot, you just have to understand that opportunities like this don't come along very often. I must do this."

I looked to the ground, not wanting Ben to see the tears forming in my eyes. I had thought we were fixed, but now it was clear that a little lust on the dance floor didn't fix anything. It just made it worse.

"You know I'll be back all the time, and, well, Dallas isn't that far away. You can come and visit me, or better yet, dump that job at the radio station and come with me." He pulled me closer. "I think I'd like that..." he nibbled on my ear. "...very much."

The thought of picking up and leaving Camden swirled through my brain. Was I ready for something like that?

The door to the Uphill opened behind us, and I took this moment to pull away.

"It's getting late. I have to work in the morning."

When I joined Ellie, she was nursing her beer. "I thought maybe you and Ben were about to get a room. I was giving you five more minutes."

"Can we go?" I said, grabbing my bag and sweater.

"Sure, but what about Ben? Where'd he go?"

"I don't know, and I don't care. As far as I'm concerned, Ben Dalton has already moved."

Chapter Twenty-Two

When I dressed for work the next day, I had an epiphany of sorts. All this wedding stuff is great, but it's not what life is about. Life is about living, not a single party on a single day. Ben dumping me had made me into a stronger woman. I didn't need to jump on the "Marry Me" train. At least not yet, and not if I wasn't ready. I felt like a grownup. At least, that's what I kept telling myself. Realistically, where would this relationship have gone? Ben was an ambitious man, and I couldn't expect him to want to stay in Camden all his life. It was a simple decision now and probably not what Sandra Dee would do. Ben could leave.

I decided I would take this time to reorganize the office because it felt like a new day. It was the same way a person reorganizes things in January as you start the new year. I was starting a new chapter of my life. I was just straightening my pin cup when Holden came out of the DJ booth.

"You're certainly industrious today."

"Sometimes it just feels good to straighten things up when you've changed your life."

Holton's eyebrow dashed up slightly. "A change? What's happened?"

We needed to keep a professional relationship between the two of us, and if we started sharing the personal details of our lives, it could put us on rocky ground. Still, as I looked into Holden's besieging eyes, it was pretty hard to resist him. He honestly wanted to know what was going on in my life. That was tremendous flattery. He leaned forward, and I could smell the Aqua Velva on him. He lowered his voice to a sultry tone and then gave me a smile. "Please don't tell me you're going to get married. I would just hate it if I had to lose you. You're the best secretary I've ever had, and the callers loved talking to you on the phone. Has some lucky guy swept you up? Do I need to look for another secretary?"

I reached over and casually patted his hand. "I'm not getting married. Just feel like organizing."

"Does this have to do with that reporter?"

"Very little."

I stood up to deposit some empty boxes into the trash can when Holden reached out and grabbed me by the waist. He pulled me in close and gave me a hug. I spoke into his shoulder. "What's this for?"

"Thank you so much for not leaving us high and dry here at KDUD. "All the while he spoke, he still held me in his arms. At the end of his last word, he pulled back slightly.

The heat between us was like the shimmering fog of a sweltering summer day on a paved road. After everything that had just happened with Ben, the last thing I wanted to do was get involved with my boss. Not only was he my employer, but his life was a mess. I needed to set things straight with him the same way I was organizing the office. "Listen, Holden. About when you kissed me at Magnolia's shower ... "

"What kiss?" Magnolia stood in the doorway in a tangerine cotton dress and matching gloves.

Holden hustled over. "Dot's a little out of her mind. Her boyfriend's leaving town. She, uh, lost control the other day and kissed me. I didn't want to tell you about it, because I didn't want to embarrass little Dot, here. She's young and didn't know what she was doing."

"What?" I couldn't believe he would resort to blaming a kiss he initiated on some sort of infatuation on my part. "You kissed me, and you know it. It's part of the reason that Ben and I broke up." I felt a little bad for striking out at him for his remark, mostly because my pain would now be Magnolia's.

"But no matter who started it," Magnolia said, her cheeks beginning to match her dress, "you two kissed."

He stumbled with his words. "It didn't mean anything." He turned to me. "Right, Dot?"

I didn't know what to say to that. It seemed like these seductions on his part kept coming up, and now I had to wonder if this marriage was a good idea.

Magnolia, who had been standing in stunned silence, finally spoke. "I don't know who's the bigger fool here. Me for wanting to marry this idiot, or you kissing him when you are supposed to be my friend. You deserve each other." She turned and made a hasty exit to the door.

Holden ran after her. "Darling, please. Forgive me. I want to marry you."

I suddenly realized that there was no music playing. Holden had left and had run out of commercials. KDUD was unmanned. I ran to the DJ booth, where Holden had the next record set up. I quickly turned on the microphone as I had seen him do and introduced the song.

"Sorry about that, folks. And now we are going to listen to a lovely song." I glanced at the record label and then threw up a sigh. Some things never changed. "Dean Martin. Enjoy." I set the record playing and turned the microphone off.

The phone in the lobby rang, and I picked up the extension in the DJ booth. "What's going on over there? Where is Holden, and why did we have dead air?" Leah had heard the gap in programming and, from her tone, was not thrilled. So, Leah listened to the radio all day. It gave me new insight into why Holden played so many oldies. It was his mother's style of music. Now I had to weigh whether I should tell her why Holden had just run out of the radio station or to make something up. I did the latter. "Holden has an upset stomach and had to run into the bathroom. He should be back soon. Luckily, he trained me on this board." Yet another lie. There was no training, and I could only do this because I had watched him do it.

"Oh dear. I should come down there and bring some medicine." Leah's tone had changed completely. It reminded me of my mother when she thought I was in trouble.

"No need for that. We have some here at the station. I'll try to keep us on the air until Holden gets back. The record is almost over. I have to go now."

I continued my unofficial DJ status. The next song he had lined up was The Andrews Sisters. Honestly, who listened to The Andrews Sisters anymore?

I glanced behind me at the bookcase full of albums. Even though they had a full library of oldies, Holden kept the top forty records and would play one every once in a while. I pulled out a Beatles album titled *Please Please Me*. As the Dean Martin song ended, I quickly switched records, lined up the needle, and came back on the microphone. "And now for something a little different. 'Listen, Do You Want to Know a Secret?' I sure do. Seems like lately, Camden is full of them. Here are the Beatles with this top-selling hit." I started the record. This was fun. I could be a DJ.

I continued to spin records of my own choosing because Holden never returned. The more music I played that wasn't a soft Perry Como ballad, the more phone calls I got. Once I put the Beatles on, I got a request for "My Guy" by Mary Wells, then "Dead Man's Curve" by Jan and Dean.

One call I found extremely rewarding. It was the DJ from KOOL, and he wasn't happy. His schoolyard bully attitude had been replaced by a grisly-sounding voice that could have been a part of organized crime. "Listen, girly, I don't know what you think you're doing over there playing DJ, but it is uncool. Or should I say you are unKOOL. Go back to playing the music to drool by, or I'll make you the laughingstock of Camden. It's Dot, isn't it? Oh, I can have loads of fun with that."

"I'll play what I want to play. You'd better hope I'm not recording this call to play on the air." As if I knew how to do that. I just hoped he wouldn't call my bluff.

The caller hung up. So, KOOL didn't like us actually competing with them, record for record. That gave me a sense of personal satisfaction. This guy had become a constant source of irritation in my days at KDUD. I was feeling like I was just going to have to put up with him, but not today. I was having a wonderful time answering the phone, playing records, and listening to my public. Much too quickly, Holden returned. I had The Everly Brothers on when he walked in, and I couldn't help but notice the jarring look he gave me. The phone rang, and I jotted another request. I had six so far on my little pad of paper and was proud of the number of phone calls I had generated during my tenure as DJ. As I finished writing the information, I noticed Holden was quietly picking up the records that I had strewn across the console, meticulously putting them back in their paper sleeves and filing them back in the cabinet. It was like I had just taken all his toys and thrown them across the room carelessly, and really, I had. It was so exciting once the calls started coming in. There wasn't time to put things away. Once I hung up the phone, Holden motioned for me to get out of the chair. He didn't like me in his territory, but he had left me no choice. There had been dead air on the radio, and that is the cardinal sin of a local radio station. It took people five seconds to find another radio station on the dial, and he knew it. At least, I think he had to know it with the outdated music selection he was putting out for the listening public. It was hard to tell with him. I had been doing him a favor. He started pulling records, and I watched the faces of Frank Sinatra, Perry Como, and Doris Day go into a stack.

"Look at all the requests we got." I held up the pad of paper filled with my excited scribbles, showing proof of my success.

Holden took it from me, then ripped off the top sheet, wadded it up, and threw it in the trash. "But people want to hear those songs," I protested.

"People don't know what they want. I have more important things to discuss. I wanted to let you know that what happened between you and me was inexcusable and that in the future, I want us to keep a professional distance. I know that working in radio is glamorous, and sometimes secretaries get crushes on DJs, but we just can't have that happening here. Do you understand?"

Why was it I felt like I was the only one who was now in the wrong for our shared kiss? I was not about to let him get away with this.

"Excuse me?"

"You heard what I said. Dot, I know you're young, but this is a business, and I need you to act professionally."

"So, what happened with Magnolia?"

He pulled at the back of his polo shirt. "Not that it's any of your business, but Magnolia and I are just fine. Once I explained your constant flirting to her, she backed off. Besides, the thought of hiring someone else for your position is too much for me to think about right now."

"Flirting? You're the one who kissed me."

"I'm sure you think that's true, but we are back on solid ground. It is especially important for my wife-to-be to prove to her family that the two of us are a good choice. I believe that's one reason she took the time to listen to the truth. I can already tell we are perfect soulmates. Now, if I can get back to work."

The record was ending as Holden sat down in the DJ chair. In his most sultry tone, he spoke into the microphone and put on a fake smile. Funny, I never noticed before just how fake it was. You could really see the crow's feet by his eyes in this light. "I'm back to rescue you from the endless rock and roll songs my little secretary, Dot, loves to play. Now let's all just simmer down and listen to 'Three Coins in the Fountain.'" He started up a record where the violins dragged me down into the abyss.

He gave me a look like he wanted me to leave, but I would not stand for him telling Magnolia that I had tried to seduce him.

He made a dismissive gesture toward the door as if I were a dog he was sending to the other room. Suddenly, my love affair with radio had become jaded. Magnolia took him back because she really wanted to marry him against her family's wishes? Just how desperately did she want to marry him? Would it be enough to take out Joyce Bishop, or had it been Holden, willing to kill her just to keep the scandal of his first wife's death out of the newspaper.

The phone rang, and I went back to doing my job.

"Is this Dot Morgan?"

"Yes, it is." The voice was familiar.

"This is Pastor Rob Roy, and I heard you on the radio. I was wondering if you could drop by my office again today."

"I suppose." I found it very puzzling that he wanted me to come back because I felt like we had discussed everything we needed to discuss. Maybe he had some other revelation to share with me. I glanced at my watch. "If I still have a job, I'll be going to lunch in about an hour." I gave Holden a nervous smile, but he didn't smile back. I returned my attention to the phone call. "Sure, I can come by."

116

Chapter Twenty-Three

When I arrived at Pastor Rob Roy's office, he was sitting behind his mahogany desk, studying his Bible.

"You wanted to see me, pastor?"

He looked up and closed the Bible. "Yes. Please sit down."

It felt like I had just been called into the principal's office. I sat in the chair in front of his desk.

"This is difficult for me to say, and I hope you'll be patient with me. Normally I would do everything I could to protect the confidence that I share with my parishioners, but—" He looked at me and slightly lowered his glasses. "I had an overwhelming rush of guilt about you, young lady."

"Me?" That was surprising. I could only hope he had finally heard himself talking about women and their tendencies toward hysteria.

"Yes, you. Every time I try to make this right in my heart, I feel like I haven't done enough. Please, pardon me for being one of the older generation who worries too much, but hopefully, I won't have to bother you again."

It was amazing to me that a man who professed his faith to others at the pulpit had so many worries about the human realm that he felt he needed to fix. Didn't that faith apply to his own life as well?

"That being said, I had a fatherly urge to tell you that you need to be careful. There are things about Holden Ramsey that you don't know." He opened up a tan folder. Inside were handwritten notes scribbled across notebook paper. "One thing I'm very good at is recording my sessions with my parishioners. That way, I can go back and remember what we talked about earlier. Everything Joyce shared with me is right here." He tapped on the paper. "All very personal and confidential and something I wouldn't want it known that this information came from me. You can understand that, can't you? Nobody is going to trust a blabbermouth minister. I know I certainly wouldn't."

Pastor Rob Roy, pillar of the community and leader of the faith, stood up.

"I'm so sorry, dear. I need to run to the restroom. Can you give me five minutes?" The way he emphasized the words, *five minutes* told me he was possibly giving me that time to look at the notes on his desk. I stood in shock as he waited patiently for my response.

I stuttered. "Of course. Take your time."

He raised his crooked finger at me. "Oh no. I think five minutes is all it should take." Pastor Rob Roy was a man who was partial to rule-following. I heard around town he was a classic fire and brimstone preacher, so this breach in his level of conduct proved to me he had weighed the options. It was more important to do the right thing, even if he had to break a rule and trip on the hot-footed path to hell. He quickly exited the room, and I stepped around his desk and read.

October 25th, 1963.

Miss Bishop is terribly upset and claims that Holden Ramsey is a dangerous person. She has given me this letter, proving how he can distort the truth.

It read:

My dearest Joyce. I'm shocked and appalled that you have miscon-strued my words and now feel that I might have pushed my first wife off the mountain where she met her death. This is of course, ridiculous, but you continue to ask me about it. It is for this reason that I am ending our relationship, and if you further pursue this, please understand that if your false accusations were to get out, it will impact my welfare, including my business and my family. Please cease and desist from flapping your gums about something that never happened. If you cannot control yourself, you will regret what you have done because of your lack of loyalty in our time together. Holden.

So, Holden was threatening her if she continued to talk about the accident his first wife had. Underneath Holden's letter was another note from the pastor.

Miss Bishop has asked me to relay this to the police, and I have. One more thing that Joyce keeps mentioning is that the atmosphere in the Ramsey house is not comfortable for her. She has spoken of being frightened at his home many times and has told me that as dashing as Holden seems to be, his home feels repressive. That was the term that she used, and I'm not sure what she was trying to express to me, but I think it's worth noting in her file. Will continue to counsel her as long as she needs it. Someone needs to be there for this girl. Her family's reputation tells me she has very few confidants.

I was just putting down the last note when Rob Roy returned. I smiled and scooted around to my side of the desk.

"Thank you so much for waiting for me, my dear. I do hope that it wasn't too dull for you."

"Not at all." It was quite revealing.

After lunch, as I sat at the desk waiting for the phone to ring, Leah came barreling in, Morris behind her. Her eyes immediately went to the DJ window. She took off her sunglasses and opened the snap lid of her purse to deposit them. "How is he doing? I've been so worried about him with everything going on and now this awful article." She turned to Morris. "Morris, give me one of my Valiums for Holden." She turned to me. "He insists on keeping them. I accidentally took too many one day. What would I do without him?" As Morris pulled a pill bottle out of his pocket, the sound of something tiny hit the floor. Had pills come out of the bottle?" Morris handed the bottle to Leah and then quickly knelt down to pick up the loose contents of his pocket.

I came around the desk. "Let me help you."

Morris held up a hand. "No need, Miss Dot. I should know better than to put birdseed in my pocket for the birdfeeder instead of putting it in a bowl. I'm afraid there are a few remnants."

Leah looked perturbed. "Morris, please quit rattling on about those birds.

You spoil them with all that expensive feed."

Morris stepped back, hands crossed in front of him. "Yes, ma'am."

I glanced at the DJ booth and then watched Leah take a pill out of the bottle. "Holden is fine. I know he's not happy, but he seems to be okay."

"Yes. That's what he does. He's such a brave man. No matter what happens to him, he always finds the strength to move on. Magnolia can count herself a lucky girl."

She made it sound like Holden was overcoming a bullet wound or something. I guess nobody loves a son like a mother. After what Magnolia witnessed this morning, I wasn't so sure about the "lucky girl" part. Magnolia had to be thinking she was making a mistake with a man whom she just caught in an embrace with his secretary. Holden's velvety voice came over the loudspeaker.

"And now let's kick it up a bit with a little Frank Sinatra." He put on "Luck Be a Lady Tonight" from *Guys and Dolls*.

Leah beamed. "Oh, my Holden. He knows I love that song. There will never be anybody as talented and handsome as Frank Sinatra." I smiled politely, thinking how cute Paul McCartney was with that bowl-shaped haircut.

Holden looked over smiled at his mother, and waved. She gave him a "good boy" look back. I had to hope that while Magnolia was counting her blessings for how strong Holden was, she should also prepare herself because Holden was the definition of a mama's boy. His perceived strength could only occur when Leah was there supporting him. He motioned for his mother to visit the booth as he turned off the microphone.

She opened the door and scurried inside.

"For you, Mother. I had to play a little blue eyes." He kissed his mother on the cheek. "What brings you here today?"

"I'm checking on you, of course. I know from the article and all, you have to be worried. How is your stomach? Dot said you were ill and had to leave your post in the DJ booth."

He looked momentarily confused, glanced my way, then took up the ruse. "You know I'm a trooper. As for the article, there's nothing they can print in that paper that's going to take me down."

CHAPTER TWENTY-THREE

"Spoken like a Ramsey."

"What else can I do?"

"If your father were here today, he would be so proud of you."

Holden's lips thinned. "I don't know about that, but it's good to know you're always in my corner." The luck was ending for Frank Sinatra and possibly Holden as the record ended.

"I'll let you get back to work. Just wanted to let you know I was thinking about you."

"Every bit helps." He gave her a grateful smile.

Magnolia called during the afternoon, and her tone was terse. I instantly connected her to Holden, trying to keep our conversation to a minimum. She was hurt, and I understood that, and after the lie Holden had told her about who started the kiss, I was surprised she wasn't pushing to have me fired. I didn't think there could be a way I could explain to her about Holden unless I told her about who he really was. In a way, I was acting like Pastor Rob Roy. I was holding back information for somebody else's own good. Near the end of the day, Holden switched out with Gerald and pulled me aside.

"Magnolia called and said she wishes to no longer have you as her maid of honor. She's planning to ask Ellie Monroe instead." Good grief. Did this girl have no friends at all?

"Why Ellie?"

"I've learned not to ask questions like that. Let's just say that with what happened, she doesn't even want to see you at the wedding."

That was rich because there were actually two people involved in the big reveal. "That's just fine with me." I snapped.

"Dot, even though what happened was unfortunate, she will be my future wife. I'll need you to respect that."

I picked up my bag. "You know, I enjoy working here, but I would ask that, as long as we're talking about respect, that you show a little my way."

"I beg your pardon?"

"You heard me. You were kissing me, or had you forgotten that part?"

"It was a moment of regret for me now, nothing more. I am a man, after all, and what you were offering so freely was hard to pass up."

Ben's kiss at the Uphill Bar was amazing, and because of it, I could feel a striking difference between him and Holden. Ben, even though he was angry after seeing me dance with Jasper, loved me. He listened to me when I explained it was just a dance, nothing more. That showed a level of trust that only formed through the friendship between us. Holden's advances were driven by pure physical attraction. He did not see me as an equal. To him, I could be told, not asked, to be a maid of honor. He saw me as young and naïve and could be seduced at his whim. Being treated equally was something Gerald and his friends had to fight for every day. I realized women had workplace rights that were also being ignored. There was a difference between mutual attraction and chasing a secretary around a desk.

Chapter Twenty-Four

That night, when I was stirring up a cup of tea and deciding that a peanut butter sandwich would make a fine meal, Ellie came storming in.

"What the hell, Dot? Magnolia Daniels says you're out as her maid of honor, and I'm in? What happened?"

"Uh, well," How could I explain this to her without making myself look like some sort of goggle-eyed teenager at her first dance? I made light of it. "She walked in, and Holden was standing very near me. I'm not sure how to tell you this, but let's just say she mistook it for something else."

"For what, exactly?"

"She thought we were kissing."

Ellie leaned back and then sat on the couch with a thud. "And now you're kissing Holden at the office?"

"It was all Holden. He hugged me, and she walked in at that moment."

Ellie's eyebrows rose, and her chin lowered. "Holden orchestrated it, and you had no part in it. That seems pretty lecherous."

"Exactly. He told me I was freely flirting with him. Another lie."

"What a creep. You know, I felt terrible when you lost your last job, but now I'm thinking there's a pattern here." Ellie sat up straighter. "Did he hurt you?"

"No. I'm fine, and I'm sorry that now Magnolia has deemed you a maid of honor."

"Like hell. I'm not going to do it. I agreed to make the woman a dress, and that's as far as my obligation is going to go."

"Did you tell her that?"

"I was too shocked, and now, because I know this is your doing, I want you to tell her."

"Me? She doesn't even want to talk to me."

"Yeah, well, you work for Holden, so she's going to have to eventually. Might as well make it sooner."

I felt my neck stiffen as I thought of approaching Magnolia. I really enjoyed working at the radio station and didn't want to be back on the job market so soon. If this kept up, I'd have to wait the counter at Woolworth's. I'd be such a pariah in the secretarial market. "Fine. You're right. You don't have to do it just because she demanded it. Someone who had been entitled their whole life thought it was appropriate to demand a wedding dress designer be a maid of honor."

"And by the way," Ellie said. "I don't think Ben is so gobsmacked by that job offer he doesn't realize what he's leaving behind."

It was only a few minutes later when Ben called.

"Hey, you want to get some dinner tonight?"

"I just ate a sandwich."

"Okay, how about I get dinner and you just nibble on something?"

"I'm not sure how I feel about that or you."

"Please, Dot? Just to talk."

"Okay, but could you come over here? Holden told me if I want to keep my job, he doesn't want me around you."

"When did he say this?"

"After the article came out. He's not too happy. Then, there's some other stuff going on, too." I was hoping Ben wouldn't ask me about the other stuff.

"Who cares about Holden?"

"I do, for now. I'm surprised you want to spend time with me, what with your job pressures and all. I have a full jar of peanut butter and bread, if you're interested."

He was at my door within ten minutes. Ellie was in her usual place at the TV, hemming away on white satin. I handed him a plate with a peanut butter and jelly sandwich, and we tried to talk in the kitchen. Unfortunately, the newest *Twilight Zone* was blaring on the TV behind us.

"Can we at least go for a walk?"

I grabbed my bag. "I know just the place."

We parked in front of the new children's park and made our way to the back, where there was a patch of woods and a trail that led into the woods. The sun was still out, and the evening breeze lifted my mood. The idea of confronting Magnolia had left a feeling of dread in me, but for this moment, I was listening to the last call of the birds and the rustle of leaves whispering on high.

"So much better." Ben strode along next to me, hands in his pockets. "I know you love your cousin, but aren't you looking forward to her moving in with Al?"

I was still mad at him from the night before, but right now, I needed a friend. The loneliness I was feeling was something I needed to get used to after Ben left and Ellie moved out. I wasn't ready for it yet, so tonight, I would let Ben back in. It would make it hurt even more when he packed up his car for Dallas, but it was like taking the last cookie on the plate. I had to have this time. "Yes, and no. I won't miss the TV watching, but I will miss having her there every night to talk to. She's not just my cousin, but my best friend."

"You'll still see her after she's married. It's not like they're leaving Camden."

"I know, but it will be different."

"I suppose." We walked onto the old wooden structure that arched over the creek. The boards were a dull gray, and it was supported by concrete cylinders on each corner. A giant live oak, its heavy branches hundreds of years old, seemed to encircle part of the bridge like a hug from the past.

Ben took my hands and blushed. "About last night…"

"It didn't end well, did it?"

"And we were doing so good until then. I'd like to get back to that if we could."

I knew he was talking about our passionate kiss on the dance floor, and even though I couldn't tell him, I felt the same way. I had to stick to my principles.

"We only stopped because you flat out told me you were leaving, and I was secondary to your job."

"Dot, it sounds awful when you put it that way. You aren't secondary to anything. We're just going to be in two cities for a while."

"Do you love me?"

"Well, yes, I have strong feelings for you. I can't deny that."

He pulled me close for a kiss, but as he did, something made me think of Magnolia's face after finding out about the kiss Holden and I shared. I turned my head.

"Gee, a guy could be very insulted looking at the frown on your face. Was it that bad?"

I looked down at the planks on the bridge. "No. I have to talk to Magnolia Daniels and explain why Ellie is not a maid of honor for hire. She dumped me when she caught Holden trying to put the moves on me in the office."

Ben paused. "He what?"

Feeling incredibly insensitive, I realized I should have told Ben this differently. "Nothing happened, but it looked bad."

"You need to quit that job." Ben's words were short, with no room for wiggling.

"No, I don't. It's a wonderful job. I can handle Holden."

"He's bigger than you, and he's your boss. There should be a law about bosses trying to seduce their secretaries."

"You're right, but if he keeps it up, I'll quit and make sure that the secretarial school blacklists him."

"Why are you staying, then?"

Why was I staying? What was there that I didn't feel like was finished? "I can't tell you, but I don't want to leave yet. Now there's this thing with Magnolia."

"There's also a murder connected to your boss, something that seems to happen to you a lot."

Leave it to a reporter to remind me of the facts I had been conveniently forgetting.

"Don't be silly. I didn't like Joyce the minute she walked into the station, but even though he could have murdered her, now I'm not so sure. Maybe that's part of the reason I'm staying. I want to prove who really took her life."

"Yes, well, there's also the angle that it had something to do with her family. They're bad news from way back. It's people like that who inspire civil rights marches."

"Gerald told me about what they did to his father. Pretty unbelievable."

Ben leaned his elbows on the railing and looked out over the water. "It also probably didn't help that Gerald and Joyce were secretly an item in high school for a while."

"What?"

"Yes, when Joyce was murdered, I started checking out her background and interviewed some of her high school classmates. She and Gerald met in secret, and it was pretty hot for a while until, I guess, Gerald couldn't get over what Joyce's father had done to his dad. It got bad between them."

"He never told me anything about that. Besides, how could he profess such a hate for them yet have a high school romance going with Joyce?"

"High school boys have been known to have misguided ideas generally coming from other parts of their bodies besides their brains," Ben answered. "The thing is, if Gerald gets named a suspect, it wouldn't go well for him."

"You're right. We already know this town's history with people that have Gerald's skin color."

It would be the ultimate revenge to kill the daughter of the man who ruined a young boy's life. I needed to look at Gerald more closely.

"Feel like going back to that club again?" I asked.

"The Uphill? Haven't you had enough of that place?"

"Guess not. I like the music."

"After what you're forced to listen to all day, I think I can understand that. All right. Let's go. Hopefully, I can get more to eat than a peanut butter sandwich."

Chapter Twenty-Five

When we entered the Uphill Bar, it was hopping. One day a week, Holden replaced Gerald with the local polka king, who also dumped Holden's records and put on an array of polka music. And then he wondered why the ratings were sinking. Searching through the haze of cigarette smoke, it took me a moment to spot Gerald over at the end of the bar, talking to a small group of men and women.

"You can really get us a record to hand out?" Asked an older man, who ran his hand through close-cut gray hair."

As Gerald was about to answer, his eyes met mine. He pulled away. "Dot? What are you doing here?"

"Uh, we just wanted to dance. What's going on?"

"Oh, nothing." He shrugged. "I'm, uh, surprised to see you here. Jasper told me you stopped by the other night, too."

"That time, it wasn't my idea. My cousin wanted to take me out after a difficult day at work."

Gerald snorted softly. "I can relate to that."

The group behind him seemed to be working ridiculously hard at minding their own business. Gerald turned away, but I grabbed his arm. "Hey, I never knew you and Joyce were an item. Why didn't you tell me?"

He tilted his head upward. "My, you have been snooping around, haven't you? Yeah, we were together. It did her old man good to find out."

"Do the police know this?"

Gerald frowned and put his mouth close to my ear. "You'd think, after the story I told you about my father, that you would have figured out by now that colored people get blamed for everything in this town. If I told the police that, they'd have me locked up before I could even call a lawyer."

Ben, who had been standing by, quietly came closer, making Gerald straighten up. "We know you're right, and we think your story should be out there fairly with no bias."

Gerald let go of my arm. "Ah, the great Ben Dalton, exposer of truth for a better Camden. Should I suppose now you're going to put that in your newspaper?"

"I don't have to. I can exercise restraint when it might cause unfair persecution."

Gerald held up a large hand and motioned in the air. "Words, all words. You think I'm going to believe that you'll hold back a big story? You sure didn't hold back on Holden Ramsey's past. Forgive me if I'm not the trusting type."

"I'm sorry," I said. "You're right. I never should have said anything." I don't know what I had been thinking. Ben had already broken one promise. He couldn't be trusted. I turned to Ben. "Please, don't print anything."

Ben looked amazed. "I said I wouldn't."

"Yeah, well, you've milked that cow one too many times." Gerald walked away in disgust. I was sad that he had to live in fear of unlawful persecution and even more sad that I might have just lost a friend.

After that, we danced, and Ben got dinner, but at the end of the evening, we hadn't come any closer to getting back to the Ben and Dot we used to be. It felt like we were simply placeholders standing in for our past.

"I'm glad we went out tonight," Ben said as he walked me to my door.

"Me too. We won't have this kind of luxury once you move away."

"That's not true. I'll be back here lots of weekends."

"That's what you keep telling me."

We kissed goodnight, but the passion of the dance floor was gone, packed up and headed out of town, just like Ben was about to do.

Chapter Twenty-Six

The next morning, when I opened the door to KDUD, I found Leah Ramsey sitting at my desk. My first instinct was to think that I had been replaced, and once she started talking, I knew I wasn't too far from the truth.

"I wanted us to have time to talk alone." She glanced at the booth. "I told the polka king to take another hour to promote his band."

Mr. Johnson was happily talking into the microphone. He had a thumb under a red embroidered suspender and a green felt hat with a feather that was cocked back slightly on his head.

"Where's Holden?"

"I told him to sleep in. After all that's happened, I think he deserves it, don't you?" Her look was steely, like she was trying to figure out what the best angle might be to shoot at me and land a kill shot. This was one of those of those moments I'll call an "as if." I stood there "as if" I wasn't mortified by her needing to talk to me.

"What can I do for you, Mrs. Ramsey?"

"I would just like to know how you ever thought it was in your favor to seduce Holden. What would there be to gain by doing this?"

"Mrs. Ramsey, it's not what you think—" I tried to explain, but she wasn't done with her own speech yet.

"Holden is engaged. That means hands off, young lady. I know you're young, and my son is very handsome, but don't worry, someday you'll find the right man. For right now, you are what I call an innocent lady-in-waiting."

I didn't have the heart to tell her I wasn't as innocent as I was last week.

She had formed an opinion, a narrative of her choosing, and she saw me as a desperate young girl eager for an older man's affections. She was right, but out of date. I had fallen for Holden's charms. He was handsome, sophisticated, charming, and, most of all, took an interest in me. Who could resist that, especially when my boyfriend had just told me he was moving on? Still, things had changed, and when Holden tried to start something the second time, I didn't want any part of it.

Leah gave me the look of a wise woman, imparting her sage impressions of what she felt I had failed to see. "Holden and Magnolia are in love, and it's a marriage that will not only benefit my son but also create a solid financial future for him."

And there it was. It was all about the money for Holden's mother. I had heard enough and interrupted her speech.

"Holden came after me, not me after him."

She pursed her lips and gave me a condescending little smile. "I'm sure you think that, but my Holden is an honorable man. No, I'm sure you wiggled that little fanny in front of him and then proceeded on down your path of seduction."

"That's not true."

"You may as well give up trying to tell me your side of the story. My son, whom I love, and trust, already filled me in on the whole incident. We sat down with Magnolia, and thank heavens, they patched things up."

I remembered how angry Magnolia had been running out the door. He might think they've patched things up, but having doubts about your husband's fidelity takes a long time to go away. I had seen it with a couple of friends. They not only didn't trust their husbands, when they moved on to another relationship, they didn't trust that person either.

"Who else knows?"

"What do you mean? This is the kind of thing one keeps within the family. Only I know and, of course, Magnolia's mother. She ran to her for comfort, but they—" She paused for a moment. "They have a unique relationship. She doesn't value Magnolia or the upcoming nuptials with my dear Holden. I'm afraid your little sexcapade made her even more resolved in trying to prevent this marriage. You should know that Magnolia now hates you and has asked Holden to fire you. He wouldn't agree on the spot, but your day is coming."

"Wonderful, and for your information, it was hardly a sexcapade. More like a boss trying to take advantage of a secretary. You know, if I really thought about this, I wonder if I could press assault charges on him."

Leah's eyes widened. "I beg your pardon. Who is going to believe you, a little secretary who was fired from her last job? Holden is a mature, accomplished member of the business community. What credentials do you have that others would believe?"

She was right. It was an obvious case of he said/she said, and he had more people who would believe him because of his position in Camden. I wasn't willing to back down, though. Leah Ramsey felt way too much-unfounded confidence in the whole situation. "Sure, I may fail, but just imagine it all getting out there. Especially with the nasty article hanging over Holden's head. Looks bad, don't you think?"

Leah's face reddened. "Listen to me, you little slut. Don't even think about doing something stupid."

Holden chose this moment to walk in, right around the word slut. "Mother? What are you doing?"

"I'm making sure that we're all on the same page about her attempt to seduce you. I'm here taking a stand for you, dear."

Holden frowned, and for the first time, I noticed it made an ugly little wrinkle right in the middle of his forehead. "Mother, I wish you would have asked me before embarking on this little meeting."

She stood up, back straight, nose pointed upward. This was the definition of a self-righteous mother. "If I had, you would have told me to stand down. I was hardly ready to do that."

Holden hunched his shoulders. "Dot, this whole incident has been unfortunate, but from now on, let's stick to purely professional office behavior. Can I hold you to that?"

The irony of him asking if he could hold me made me want to laugh out loud.

"Sure, boss," I said, pulling my lips in to prevent a smile. At least he didn't fire me. Getting fired from two jobs in a row would spell the beginning of my next career. Maybe I could get a crossing guard job or be a dog walker.

The rest of the day went by uneventfully, and I thought my ears would melt off my head if I kept hearing 101 Strings slow down every song ever written. Holden was in an instrumental mood, which must have bothered his mother, waiting to hear her crooners. I guess when you are in your forties, it's harder to rebel against a parent.

That night, I expected Ben to call, but he didn't. His move was getting closer; all the while, he was trying to write stories to impress Dallas. I told myself I didn't mind. I was tired after all the drama going on in my life and settled down to sleep at about 9:30. Ellie was still up watching *Gunsmoke* when I said good night.

Three hours later, people were yelling in my dreams, but I couldn't understand them. Whatever it was, the voice was upset. What were they saying? Flower? They wanted flowers? When I opened my eyes, Ellie's face was squared up to mine, and I realized she was yelling at me.

"Fire! Get out of bed! The house is on fire!"

Chapter Twenty-Seven

I couldn't think, couldn't see, did not know what to grab besides my cousin. I put my feet in slippers, grabbed my robe from the end of the bed, and felt Ellie pulling me out of the apartment. The billows of smoke were everywhere, but I couldn't see any fire in our tiny home. As I tried to breathe, I coughed and covered my mouth with the lapel from my robe. When we got to the stairs, the fire made a grand entrance, licking around the front door of Arlene's house.

"Where's Arlene?" I asked.

"I don't know." Ellie looked around and yelled, "Arlene?"

I followed suit and yelled Arlene's name as we descended the stairway and made our way to the kitchen and the back door. Every time I yelled out, I exposed my lungs to the ashy air and coughed. "We have to check her room. She might still be asleep." A board crashed behind us, and a fire engine wailed in the distance. We found Arlene asleep, and whether she was there because she was truly asleep or suffering from smoke inhalation, I couldn't be sure. Ellie began yelling again, pulling Arlene up from the sheets, giving her much the same treatment I had received.

Arlene, her curlers neatly aligned on her head like little pink soldiers, raised a large pudgy hand and tried to bat Ellie away like an irritating insect.

"Arlene," I joined Ellie, trying to rouse her. "The house is on fire. Get up."

Arlene sat straight up and then with speed I never would have thought of a woman her age, was at the door in an instant. "My pictures. I have to get my pictures." She ran in the fire's direction to the living room, the smoke now a thick fog around us.

"No, we have to get out," Ellie yelled.

"No. I have to get them." She felt along the bookshelf and grabbed three scrapbooks. "Take these." She threw them at me and then grabbed more. "Let's go." She walked past me with her books, and I followed, feeling some frustration she'd slowed our escape but was also amazed at her quick thinking.

Once outside, the neighborhood was lit up like Christmas Eve between the lights on the fire engine and the fire itself. Mary ran up, a sweater over a nightgown and pair of pants. *"Madre di Dios,* you're okay. Someone from the station called me."

She hugged me, and as I fell into her embrace, Ben came running up, camera around his neck, his pajama pants and slippers sticking out from under his trench coat.

Mary pulled away, and Ben took me in his arms.

"Dot! Thank God. When the newspaper called and gave me the address, I didn't even change clothes," he whispered into my hair. "I could have lost you, just like that."

Another round of coughs hit me. "My parents. I need to call my parents." I didn't want to let go of Ben and the security I felt with his arms around me.

Mary patted me on the back. "I'll take care of it."

People were coming from everywhere now. Al pulled up in his electric truck, parking askew, causing a bit of a traffic snarl. His long legs crossed the parking lot in record time, and then he grabbed Ellie. Arlene was now sitting on the back end of the ambulance, being taken care of by Homer Peterson, one of the town's doctors. Homer had to be near seventy, but still went out on house calls. He was now delivering babies from babies he delivered decades ago. The ambulance driver stood by, ready to transport anyone who needed help to the hospital.

The fire department was near to putting out the flames that had centered mostly on the front porch. What up there might have caused a fire? It had been a screened-in porch that Arlene loved to read in on temperate afternoons. It was a room of books and plants.

More people surrounded Arlene, and I was surprised to see Morris, the

Ramsey's man, there with a couple of blankets and a look of concern. He came over and offered me one.

"I must confess, I listen to the police scanner at night. I'm an old man, and I find it thrilling. I didn't know you lived in this home with your cousin from the dress shop. You're just lucky your neighbor delivers papers early in the morning."

I took the blanket, now feeling strangely cold even though it was late May in Texas. "Thank you, but I don't think Mrs. Ramsey would be too happy to see you helping the enemy."

Morris cocked his head slightly. "What Mrs. Ramsey doesn't know won't hurt her." He looked back at the house. "Do they have any idea how it started?"

"I don't know. I'm still trying to get over the fact that it started, and I don't think I'm ready to think how," I answered.

Ben spoke. "Have you heard anything? I'm a reporter for the *Camden Courier.*"

Morris barely gave Ben time to finish his sentence as his words cut in. "Yes, I believe someone told me that. I haven't heard anything but will be eager to know what you find out."

"If you're all right, I'll go start working on the story." Ben gave me a quick kiss and walked away.

First, the story, then me. I pulled the blanket closer and saw Gerald standing on the edge of the crowd. He didn't look like he was rendering aid anywhere, and I had to ask myself what he was doing here. Was the whole town listening to their police scanners?

Morris gave a little bow. "I should go see if I can help anyone else." He gave me a curious little smile and walked off into the melee of people now gathered on our quiet street.

Aunt Mavis, Ellie's mother, marched onto the scene wearing a bathrobe, curlers, and green rubber garden boots. Behind her were who she called her "Gal Pals," Rosie Finebaum and Eula Beth Murray. Rosie was the only Jewish person in town, and Eula Beth and Mavis had one of the few black/white friendships. One distinction that drew them together was they had all served in the Waves in World War II. Mavis had been a nurse, Eula Beth a cook, and Rosie filed paperwork for the troops.

When Aunt Mavis came into a room, people sat up straighter and paid attention. She demanded it. That was why Ellie worked so hard in her dress shop. She had been raised by a Drill Sargent of a mother who did not put up with foolishness. Ellie's mother wasn't pleased when she announced her Peace Corps plans last year. Fail to plan and plan to fail, she would always say. It also couldn't be denied that, for all her gruffness, she was still a mother. Losing her daughter for any amount of time was too much of a cost.

"Where's Ellie?" she asked, forgoing the "Hello, how are you, Dot?"

"She's around somewhere."

She turned to Rosie. "Fan out, girls, and find Ellie. We need to establish that she is all right."

Without a word, Rosie and Eula Beth scattered. Mavis turned her attention back to me. "What the hell happened here? Was someone burning a candle? You know how unsafe they are."

"No, Aunt Mavis. At least, I don't think so."

She gave a stiff nod. "Good. Glad to hear it. Does your mother know you got out okay?"

Even though her words were kind, they were still delivered with a gruff sensibility.

"Mary is calling them." I shook under the blanket. "It happened so fast." Aunt Mavis put her arm around me.

"Just glad you're safe, kid. These things happen like that."

Eula Beth walked up with Ellie on her arm. "Found her. She was trying to get back into the house."

Mavis left me and went to Ellie. First, she hugged her only daughter. Both women were tall, but somehow, Mavis was taller. After the hug, she stepped back. "Don't ever go into a house that's still on fire. You can get whatever you need later if it's still there. Human life is much more precious than any kind of baubles you may have."

Ellie ran a hand under nose, causing the soot on her cheek to spread to her ear. "Not baubles, mama. I had a wedding dress I was working on up there."

"Listen, kid, even if it didn't burn up in the fire, you'll never get the smell of smoke out of it. Write it off," Mavis said, and then she drew her daughter back in. "So glad you're okay." She shut her eyes as if to stop a tear but wasn't successful in her effort.

Chapter Twenty-Eight

The next morning, I called in sick, still shaken up from the fire. I found comfort sleeping at my parents' house, hearing the neighbor mowing, smelling bacon, and the low hum of my parents' voices. It was what I needed right now. I pulled the old pink and yellow appliqued tulip quilt up to my chin. My grandmother had made it for me and given it to me on my tenth birthday. She told me a girl with a spring birthday needed tulips all year long. If I could just stay here, I would be safe and warm, and if I ventured downstairs, I'd be well-fed. No Holden, no Ben, no visions of Joyce on the pet store floor. I was just drifting off when there was a gentle tap on my door.

"Dot, dear. Are you awake?" My mother had also taken the day off from the library to be with me. I tried to tell her I was fine, but she insisted, and, really, I wasn't that fine.

"Yes."

"I'm sorry to bother you, but you have a visitor." Her hand was still on the doorknob, and she looked down the hallway. "He's downstairs."

"Is it Ben?" I felt a mixture of surprise and an unexpected rush of happiness. I thought he would have rushed to the newsroom to type up the story of the big fire at Arlene's house. I was more important. My letting him go so easily was a mistake.

"No. It's a fellow from work. His name is Gerald?"

Of all the people I expected to check on me, Gerald was not even in the top ten. We had left each other on such a sour note, and I felt bad about that. Still, I couldn't deny that seeing him at the fire was strange. There were

139

things about Gerald I had chosen to ignore. Why would he be there, and why did he run off when I noticed him? I grabbed my robe, and the smell of smoke assaulted my nose. It had permeated the fibers. It was so ghastly I couldn't put it on.

My mother held out her hand. "Here, let me try to wash that. I don't know if we can even get that smell out." I think you have an old robe in the closet." I gave a shaky grin and handed it over, reveling because no matter what happens in life, your mom will still take your problems and throw them in the wash for you.

Gerald stood at the bottom of the stairs, hat in hand.

"Hello, Dot. How are you doing?"

"I'm still a little shaken. I hope everything is okay at the station."

"As good as it ever will be."

"Good. Would you like some coffee? My mother always has a pot going."

"Sure."

I led him into my parent's kitchen. I quickly put together two mugs of coffee and joined him, now seated at the kitchen table. "I saw you last night. At the fire."

He nodded. "Yeah, I thought you did."

"What were you doing there?"

He took a sip and then quietly set his mug on the table. "I don't know. I came over after work and was trying to get up enough nerve to talk to you. I stood outside your house for a while."

"Doing what?"

"Getting up my courage. I wanted you to help me talk to Holden. I've been using his studio for a while now, and people are lining up to record there. The problem is, people don't want to sneak in and record in the middle of the night. I need to use the studio during the day. Plus, well, there's some equipment that needs to be replaced if I'm going to keep recording people."

I raised my cup to my lips and took a drink. The coffee was good and strong. "You think Holden is going to listen to me?"

He snorted. "You think he's going to listen to me? Dot, you got the in. He doesn't like my music, and I don't think he cares too much for me. If he had it his way, there'd be some white gent in there spinning records."

"That's not true."

"It is, and you know it."

"Yes, well, he just lied to his mother and everyone else that I was coming on to him at work. He wasn't exactly wanting to buddy up with me when I tried to tell everyone different."

Gerald hit the table with the heel of his hand. "I knew it! I could feel it in the air. That old dog. Typical Holden."

"To be fair, I thought he was very handsome."

"Handsome. Charming. Those are his weapons. He wields them on everyone, and you, little girl, were not immune. Now he's blaming it all on you. Why?"

"Because Magnolia caught him trying to kiss me. I probably shouldn't tell you this, but I let him kiss me at Magnolia's shower."

"My, my. You have been busy."

"Yes, but I pulled away as soon as it happened. Unfortunately, Ben saw it."

"Dot, Dot, Dot. Here I am thinking you're Gidget when I should have been seeing you as Marilyn Monroe." He laughed softly, then a serious look blanketed his features. "Listen to me. Keep your distance from that guy. Don't you let Holden blame you for something you didn't do. Speaking from experience, once somebody blames someone else, half the people listening get reeled in on the lie."

I thought of Gerald's father. I bet more than half believed Mr. Bishop's lie about him. "Thank you."

"It's that reason I also want to ask you, not to mention to the police that you saw me at the fire. You know, the first person they'll suspect will be me. Especially if they find out, you asked me about Joyce. If Ben puts it in the paper, I'm done for."

I was about to agree when a question came into my mind. Why couldn't it be him? If he was the person who killed Joyce, then fire would be a way to stop my meddling. "I'll try not to, Gerald, but if anyone asks directly, I have to tell the truth."

"I suppose." He ran a hand over his forehead. "One thing you should know.

I was hanging back by that old cottonwood tree and saw someone sneak up on your porch."

"You did? Who was it?"

"Don't know. They were dressed in dark clothing, and I couldn't even tell you if it was a man, woman, fat or skinny. I didn't dare get any closer. They opened the porch door, and the next thing I knew, they ran off down the stairs, and a little flame started up. I should have called the police, but I was sure they'd blame me. I just hope you can understand that. Whoever this was, I don't think your life was important."

He saw the arsonist. Could he be lying about that, too? I felt guilty for doubting him, but I had too many facts swirling around in my memory. I didn't know who to trust.

After Gerald left, I went back to Arlene's to pick up a few things. Hopefully, I'd be able to move back after a few days. When I got there, Ellie was loading her car with dresses from the shop.

"They're ruined." She shook her head in disgust.

"They look okay to me." They didn't even have soot marks on them. That meant the fire never got into our apartment, soon to be my apartment only.

"Sure, but they smell like smoke. What bride is going to want one of these dresses in their wedding?"

"Is there a way to get the smoke out?"

"Your mother told me to use baking soda. Put the dress in a bag with a bunch of baking soda, shake it, and let it set overnight. I'm willing to try it, but I doubt it will work. Between the time I put into them and the cost of the material, this is going to be an enormous loss."

I looked over at the house. The fire department had successfully stopped the damage, going no further than Arlene's front porch. It looked funny now, with parts of the house exposed to the street. Ellie followed my gaze.

"She's got Rabbit Stephenson coming this morning to start work. He thinks he can have a new porch back on within the month. What about you? Are you going to move back in?"

"In a few days. I just came to get some stuff."

"I was already packing, so I don't have much to move out. Let's just say Al is pretty happy I'm moving in a few days before the wedding."

"Oh my, what will the gossips say?"

"That they were right all along." She laughed and closed her door on a crinoline.

Chapter Twenty-Nine

Monday morning, I made it a point to arrive a little early for work. If Holden was on the edge of firing me, being late would not be the reason. When I walked in, he was playing "Someone to Watch Over Me," as orchestrated by Roger Williams, another song that was nowhere near the Billboard Top Ten. He should have been playing "My Guy" by Mary Wells, "Love Me Do" by the Beatles, or even "Hello Dolly" by Louis Armstrong. It seemed like the more trouble he got into with his mother, the more of her favorite songs got played on the radio.

Around noon, Magnolia came in wearing a white sleeveless dress with a scalloped collar, and in her hair, she had placed a small black hat with a bow. She wore short white gloves, and there was a sparkling bracelet with a small gold pendant attached to it. Her brown locks had a flip on the end, making her look like a page out of McCall's. If she had made eye contact with me, I would have told her how stylish I thought she looked, but she flitted past me with nary a word. As she removed her white gloves, she turned the doorknob to the DJ booth.

Holden, who was in the middle of talking, smiled and held up a hand, directing her out of the booth. Magnolia backed out and then, with a slight frown, returned to the lobby.

"Can I get you some coffee?" I asked.

"No. I didn't plan to speak to you today. I certainly hope you've been able to keep your hands off my fiancé this morning."

Just in case I had harbored the notion that Magnolia didn't trust Holden's side of the story, she was proving she believed in him and not me. I don't know what I expected. She *was* engaged to him. It was amazing to me she was so loyal even after hearing Joyce's claims. "It wasn't like that."

"So, you say. Holden and I had a long talk, and I now understand what happened much better. I know he's a handsome man, but that doesn't mean he's available."

"I wasn't…" She didn't let me speak.

"The worst part of all of this was you gave my mother another weapon to use against me. She dislikes Holden, and this incident gave her a reason to once again forbid me to wed him."

"I'm sorry to hear that—"

"The thing is, through all of this, I've realized that now I want to marry him just to spite my mother. She's always hated everything I do, so why not? When the station takes off, and Holden is wildly successful, that will be all I need to show her. She's a controlling, unreasonable woman."

"That seems harsh."

"You do not know what I've been through with her. When the thing about Joyce came out in that rag of a paper, my parents were furious. Frankly, I'm glad Joyce is dead. Her being pushed out of the way signaled things finally going right in my life. It's about time."

As the haunting trumpet of "Cherry Pink and Apple Blossom White" came over the speaker, Holden stepped out. Magnolia put on a pouty face.

"There you are. I thought you were going to stand me up for the final cake tasting."

Holden pushed up the knot in his tie. "Never, my darling." He turned to me. "I'll be gone for about an hour. I'm leaving you in charge of the DJ booth, but…"

He drew his eyebrows together. "You will play nothing but the records I have stacked next to the turntable. Is that clear?"

I was happy I was going to get back to the DJ booth, but the idea of playing music to sleep by was not my idea of fun. "Sure. Only the records by the record player. Got it, boss."

I got myself settled in and loaded up the next record. Holden left me some news to read, and there at the top was Arlene's fire.

"Hello there, Dot Morgan back on the air while the boss heads off to eat cake. Here's the news. There was a fire at Arlene Clark's a couple of days ago. The front porch was consumed, but all occupants of the home got out alive." I looked away from the script. "I can tell you personally that everyone got out alive because I was in that fire. Thank goodness for my roommate Ellie Monroe for waking me up in the nick of time, but there's more to this than a three-line story before moving on to the sports scores. This fire was no accident. No, someone set it. Why do I think this, you ask? Because this person was witnessed sneaking onto the front porch and then running out after lighting a small flame. Right now, you're thinking you've gotten away with this, but you won't. Who saw you? Mums the word. The next record I play should be "Great Balls of Fire," don't you think? Nope. The boss left me "Only You" by the Platters. It could be that song works, after all. Who set the fire? Only you."

After that, I put the record on and sat back. I enjoyed being a DJ. I enjoyed having a voice that others would hear. No wonder Holden loved it so much.

When Holden came back, I had played almost every record on the stack and begrudgingly returned to my desk. When Gerald came in at 4:30, he had a look of determination on his face. I had forgotten he asked me to help him sway Holden into getting to use the recording studio.

"You ready for this?" he asked.

"I don't know. Holden's been grumpy all day. This thing with Magnolia has him on edge."

"Come on, Dot. I need to replace that equipment. If we don't ask, we'll never know."

"I suppose you're right." I wrote a quick note asking to talk for a few minutes and left it by Holden's side in the booth.

"And now I have a treat for you. We're going to hear a double of Frank Sinatra. 'Fly Away with Me' and 'Luck Be a Lady Tonight.'" He put the needle on the record and stepped out of the booth.

"You wanted to talk to me, Gerald?"

Gerald rubbed his hands on his thighs. "Yes. I'll be quick. You see…" Gerald stopped. He was nervous, and it seemed to have stopped his tongue from working.

I stepped up. "Gerald has been using the studio, and it's been a big hit. Isn't that exciting?"

The expression on Holden's face wasn't anywhere near excited. "You what? You used the studio without my permission? I thought we had this talk already."

Gerald held up a hand as if stopping the negativity coming off Holden. "Hear me out, Holden. Yes, we discussed it, but I decided to just try it once. It was so successful I had bands coming from all around that wanted to record."

"How many recordings have you made?"

He looked up and put a hand on his forehead. "I'd say about seven. After we record the songs, I send them to a record company in Nashville who makes copies for us."

"How much are you charging these people while you're stealing the use of my equipment?"

"Not much. Like I said, I was just experimenting at first. But now, I can see this is a suitable business model, and we could use it to keep the station afloat."

I thought using the recording studio to boost income at the station was a great idea. There was no way anyone was listening to us while we played Leah's favorite hits.

"How long has this been going on?" Holden asked.

"Just since March."

"I see." Holden walked over to my desk and took off a sheet of paper from my notepad. "Figuring costs to use my equipment and rental of the space, " He jotted down some numbers. "Hmmm. I would say you owe me around $500. You're right. We could use a cash infusion right now."

Gerald's eyes widened. "Are you kidding?"

"Nope."

"That's a bit steep, isn't it?"

"Wouldn't know. I've never rented out a recording studio before."

"I guess I could hit up the recording artists to see if they'll pay for this. We have another group coming in tonight for a session."

"Oh, no, you don't. You don't use that studio until you pay the $500. As long we are talking about recording artists," Holden stressed the last two words, and not in a good way. "I'm supposing they look like you."

Gerald folded his arms across his chest and jutted out his chin. "They do. It's very hard for colored groups to get a recording time in Dallas. That's just another reason we need to use your studio."

"I don't think so. If they can't get time in Dallas, there must be a reason. I'm thinking they must be hard on the equipment."

"They can't get time because they're colored. People in Dallas are racists."

"Excuse me?"

"You heard what I said. I certainly didn't think I'd be applying that term to you, but now I see that I'm wrong."

"You'd better watch out what accusations you're throwing around. I can get someone else to take your time slot on the radio."

Chapter Thirty

Gerald was a different man after his meeting with Holden. After checking around Dallas, we found our boss was charging too much for using the studio. Gerald called it the "colored" tax.

Gerald paced the floor. "I kept trying to think the best of the man, but in the end, he's just like all the rest."

"Is there anyone you could go to and complain about this?"

"Who would that be exactly? A white cop? A white judge? There's nobody there who can help us. The best thing we can do is to come up with the money." He paced around the office, and when I glanced at the DJ booth, I could see Holden watching us. I grabbed Gerald by the arm, and we stepped out of Holden's view.

"What are you going to do?"

Gerald shook his head from side to side, but then stopped. "What am I going to do? There's a difference between me and Holden, and I'm not just talking about the color of our skin. That man in the booth doesn't have any friends except his mother and his fiancée, and neither of them has too many either. I have the pleasure of working with a lot of good people. You never know until you ask, right?"

He was right. I'd seen the crowd at the Uphill Bar. They were tight-knit and kind people.

"You can start with me." I walked back into the office, opened my purse, and pulled out a twenty. Holden glared through the window. I simply smiled back and placed the money in Gerald's hand. "I know it isn't much…"

He put his hand over the money and then mine. "Coming from you, in front of him, it means the world to me, Dot Morgan."

I had big hopes for Gerald paying off Holden, but he deserved more. I pictured what the station would be like if Gerald were to run it. The first thing that would go would be all those old fifties ballads. I had already experimented with a different playlist, and once I did, the phone started ringing. I had never asked much about what Holden did before KDUD. Had he run other stations? Most of the goings on in this station seemed scrapped together between him and his mother.

After Gerald left to get some supper before he went on the air, a quiet fog of nothingness fell over the station.

The phone rang, and I answered with the written script, but the voice on the other side didn't sound right.

"You need to stop playing that music at night. No decent people around here want to hear that."

I knew he was referring to Gerald's music programming. The voice was familiar.

"Who is this?" I asked.

"Never you mind who this is. You've been warned. If we wanted to hear Stevie Wonder, we'd go to Detroit or Chicago. Leave off on that garbage."

As the caller went off the line, I realized whose voice it was. It was the DJ over at KOOL, but this time, he didn't sound like he was making me the butt of a joke. This time he sounded angry and a scary kind of mean. So, they made fun of the music Holden played and hated the music Gerald played. What a jerk.

I was concerned because he was calling with a warning to stop playing Gerald's music. What did he plan to do? I had just been through a fire and was terrified to think about being in another one. I had seen a cross burning one time when we were out in the country. My father said it was a hateful act of stupid people. He told me it is better to love others who differ from you than to hate them for their differences. That was what made the world exciting and whole. Would fire be the KOOL DJ's idea of punishment? He didn't seem to have the intellectual capacity to be original in his thoughts.

As I placed the phone back on the receiver, I debated whether I should tell Holden about the phone call. He was already overcharging Gerald for something he wasn't even using. Holden didn't know how to use the studio because if he did, he might realize it was another revenue stream for the station. Advertisers were getting fewer and fewer, and the music was getting slower. I wasn't even sure if he was playing the records at the right speed. I went back to my thoughts on the KOOL DJ. I should probably tell Holden, but I decided I could put it off for a day or two. Let this thing about the studio settle down first. The phones went back to quiet, causing me to put time in on an intricate doodle of Ellie's face when she told me about the fire. Happy to hear a ring break the boredom, I answered right away.

It was Magnolia, and she was crying. "Can you cover the booth?"

"Yes. Magnolia, are you okay?"

"Obviously not. My parents have forbidden me to marry Holden, and I need you to tell him." She broke into a sob.

"Me? Why not you?"

"Because they told me I'm to never see him again."

This was confusing, because I thought this was solely her decision, and she didn't care what her parents, specifically her mother, felt about the situation. "Why now?"

"Because they've threatened to do to me what they did to my brother. They'll cut me off. Make me move out. Make me get a job and support myself. This can't be happening."

"But you knew that was a risk."

"Yes," she sniffled. "But, I never thought they'd actually carry it through. They sent the maid in today to pack my things into boxes. They said if I continue with this marriage, I need to be out by five p.m. today." With that, she went into a full-blown crying jag.

I wasn't exactly Holden's favorite person right now, and the thought of informing him he'd been dumped would not help me any. "Listen, Magnolia, let me put you through to him, okay?" Before she could protest, I transferred the call to the booth. Holden, who had been arranging records, reached over and answered. I was sure she had hung up, but he instantly smiled upon hearing her voice. As I watched, the smile reversed, and he lowered his head as he listened to Magnolia. Suddenly, he looked up and repeated the word "Hello." When he slammed down the receiver, I knew Magnolia had ended the call. He grabbed his jacket and came bounding out of the booth.

"Take over. I don't know when I'll be back."

As he whooshed out the door, I recognized the sound of the stereo needle looping back and forth on the empty space on the record. I ran to the booth and quickly turned on the mic.

"Dot Morgan here, taking over for the boss again." There was copy for a commercial in front of me, so I began reading and reset the needle on a different song on the album. Once the song was playing and the mic was off, I looked around for some of the Beatles records I had played before, but they were not filed where they had been on the shelf. My suspicions were Holden had purposely moved them to prevent me from a rock and roll takeover. Under the back table, I found a box with Gerald's name on it. When I pulled it out, I found plenty of records and quickly put one aside.

As the other recording finished, I turned on the microphone. "'The Days of Wine and Roses.' What a classic. Speaking of which, our favorite dressmaker at Bluebonnets Dress Shop is getting married this Saturday. This next song is a little tribute to her and Al, the man who really gets her electricity going. 'Just Like Romeo and Juliet,' by the Reflections." Within two minutes, the phone rang. I answered the first line while the second line lit up. I jotted a request for "My Guy" and then went to the second line.

"Dot Morgan, you just announced my wedding over the radio!" Ellie was on the other end.

"Yes, but I didn't say where, so you're fine."

"You think everyone in this town doesn't know where? There aren't that many choices."

"Sorry."

"Yeah, well, when Al hears that little electric joke, he's the one who's going to want an apology, although it was kind of funny." She giggled. What a relief she wasn't angry with me. The first line rang again. I said goodbye and clicked the button.

"What is going on over there?" It was Leah. "Why isn't my son on the radio?" I eyed the record and quickly pulled out a Nancy Wilson album and readied it.

"He had to leave suddenly."

"I realize he's not there. Where did he go?"

I wasn't sure just how much to reveal. "Magnolia called, and he told me to take over the booth."

"What about?"

"You'll have to ask him. I couldn't say." What I meant was I shouldn't say, or better yet, I wouldn't dream of letting you know your son's wedding just crashed. Hopefully, he would patch it up and Leah would never be the wiser. From my observation, she was the mother you didn't want handling crisis management because she made things worse, not better.

"I know you're holding something back. You might be a petite little blond, but you are not the harmless facade you put forth. You have a way of getting involved in other people's business."

"I don't know what you're talking about."

Leah snorted, "I think you do." There was a pause, and I quickly set the second record to play. "If he ran to Magnolia, I'll assume he went to her house. Am I close?"

"Again, Mrs. Ramsey, he just ran out of here. I don't know which way he went."

"If I find out that the wedding is in trouble because of that article in the paper, the only job you'll be able to get in this town before the week is out will be a carhop." She hung up and hoped, for my sake, she was wrong. I was a lousy skater.

Chapter Thirty-One

That night, we had a planning meeting before the wedding. Even though Ben was leaving town, he was still slated to be the best man for Al, so we met at the VFW Hall, where they would hold the reception. Ben informed me he had left the location of our dinner with his paper just in case anything broke on the Joyce Bishop case. We parked downtown about a block from the hall. We walked past Animal Kingdom, which was still open. Ben touched my arm. "That's her father."

"Joyce's?"

A man with a thick waist was pulling paper out from under a birdcage, scattering birdseed on the ground. I thought of everything Gerald had told me about him wrongly imprisoning his father.

"I want to talk with him." Ben started toward the door. Didn't he have any sense of wariness after a murder was committed in that store? I had to stop him.

"No, you don't. He's a dangerous man."

Ben, who had been focused on the man in the window, now turned to me with a curious stare. "What do you know about him?"

"He committed a crime and blamed it on somebody else. You know that."

"Yes, but he also just lost his daughter. Have a little compassion for that."

Ben was right, but any man who would send another man away for his crime didn't rate high in my book. Ben stepped into the pet shop as the shop owner looked up from his job.

"Mr. Bishop?" Ben asked.

"Who wants to know?" Wyatt Bishop didn't look trustful of his fellow man, and as he spoke, his head twisted slightly, causing a double chin to form on one side.

"Ben Dalton, *Camden Courier*."

"I got nothing to say to you." The bird, as if in accord, gave a shrill chirp that bounced off the quiet walls of the pet shop.

"I understand. I just wanted to share my condolences on the loss of your daughter, Joyce. I never actually met her, but we crossed paths the night before she died."

"You did?" Wyatt looked genuinely surprised, but I wasn't so sure that was a good thing for Ben. They hadn't yet established who killed her, and here he admitted that he, a man her father didn't know, had been around her the night before her murder.

Bishop placed fresh paper in the cage. "How did your paths cross?"

Ben cleared his throat. He didn't look comfortable when someone else was asking the questions. "Um, we were at Columbo's the night your daughter came in and accused Holden Ramsey of murder in front of everyone."

Wyatt pressed his plump lips together and swallowed. "Holden Ramsey. Now there's a dandy for you. I don't know what she saw in that man. Did you know his mother bought him another radio station that he ended up ruining? He's a born loser."

That was intriguing. I had wondered if Holden had always been in radio. "Were there other radio stations?"

"One. He took over a country station for a while, but when he refused to play Hank Williams or any of those fellas, his audience dwindled, and they went out of business."

Funny how that was the same pattern I saw happening at KDUD. Before Holden bought it, I remember listening to KDUD in high school. They played top hits, not old standards. How much had his mother played a part in these failures to produce consistent listeners?

"Yep. He can't do anything without his mama. My Joycee never got fair treatment out of him. She told me she felt like a stand-in while he searched for someone with more money. His first wife had plenty of it, you know. When she died, she left him a pile of cash, and that's part of how they bought

KDUD. Pretty damn convenient, don't you think?"

How could a man as handsome and charming as Holden be such a snake? I couldn't decide if I should believe Mr. Bishop or write him off to the same conspiracy theory Joyce attested to. It also added fuel to the theory that having the wedding canceled would be a terrible thing for Holden, who couldn't stop screwing up in the eyes of his mother.

I had to think there was more to this. "Uh, I work at the radio station, and your daughter accused Holden of murdering his first wife in front of me and the night DJ."

Wyatt started to say something and then suddenly stopped. "Night DJ? You don't mean that Watson boy, do you?"

I had forgotten the connection between Joyce and Gerald and regretted what I had just said. This would stir up even more emotions in Wyatt. I tried to minimize the damage. "Uh, yes. Gerald Watson."

He blew out a stale breath. "I should have known he would be involved. Wherever that family goes, they cause trouble. We been laying low, trying not to attract that kind. The thought of him and my Joycee in the same room..." His cheeks grew red. "Leave. I'm done talkin'."

The VFW Hall was crowded when we got there. Al was a veteran, so we could order at the bar. Ellie knew this place well, not only because of Al but because it was a regular hangout for Aunt Mavis and her gal pals. Uncle Howard was smaller Aunt Mavis in every way. He was shorter, sweeter, and quieter. She was a take-charge kind of gal, where he was bookish and very in love with his wife. Uncle Howard had delivered milk for as long as I'd known him. He once told me he loved the quiet of the early mornings. Tonight, though, Mavis was nowhere to be seen. She and the gal pals had a bowling team. This was their night at the Lone Star Lucky Lanes.

"Sorry we're late," I said as I took the seat, Ben had pulled out for me at the table. "Walter Cronkite here spotted Joyce Bishop's father and had to interview him."

"As in the dead woman? What did he say?" Al asked.

"He doesn't think a lot of Holden Ramsey and called him a mamma's boy.

He also didn't think much of his daughter's choice in men."

"Ah, yes, mothers are the root of all stress some days. I certainly know mine is right now," Ellie said, circles under her eyes.

"Your mom is great. What are you talking about?" I asked.

"She isn't great when her only daughter is getting married. It's like it's her wedding some days. She's constantly calling me to make sure I've done everything." Ellie turned to Al. "What was the last one?"

Al, elbows on the table, had his chin on these hands. "Shoes. She wanted to make sure I shined my shoes."

"God forbid Al walks down the aisle with unpolished shoes."

Al nodded. "Kind of reminds me of my old drill sergeant, sometimes."

Ben laughed. "Better get used to it, Al. You get Ellie's mother for life. You are now officially a part of her battalion, Soldier."

"I was afraid you'd say that." Al turned to Ellie, who wasn't laughing. It's one thing to insult your mother, but quite another if somebody else insults her. Even if it's the man you love.

"I don't care how many times she calls. I love your mom. She was there for me after the fire. She loves you too, and well, she's always been a take-charge kind of mother."

"And I wondered where Ellie got it from," Al added.

"I just can't wait until all of this is over and we can get back to our normal lives." The manager came over to the table as Ellie finished her sentence.

"Excellent. We're so glad you came by to settle up the final details." The manager of the VFW was a former four-star general, who always made me think of the song from White Christmas, "What do you do with a general when he stops being a general?" You let him run the local VFW Hall.

"I think you'll find our hall in tip-top shape. We will, of course, go out of our way for a vet, right Al?"

"Yes sir," Al replied automatically. From there, Ellie and Al discussed the reception details. As they walked away, Ben and I sat quietly at the table.

There was so much unsaid between us. He was officially leaving after the wedding, and since we had parted ways, it was like the time that stretched until the goodbye was lasting forever. I wished it was next Monday, and Ben was off looking for his big story, while I settled back into some quiet days to think about everything. So much had changed. I had changed and proven to myself that, at least, I thought so. All he was thinking about was his big break to Dallas. I was yesterday's news.

Ben cleared his throat. "This is exciting, but it feels like it's the end of an era. Like the last day of high school or something. Do you feel it?"

I smiled. "Yes. It's going to be pretty lonely."

"That it is," he agreed. I had to wonder if he was talking about my losing Ellie or losing him. He breathed in quickly and spoke. "Listen…. I just wanted to say…."

"I think we're all set," Ellie said from behind us. Ben stopped talking. The moment had passed.

"Great," he said, glancing at his watch. "I'd better get going. Busy day tomorrow." He stood and then gave me a perfunctory kiss. He raised a hand and waved. "It's going to be great." He walked out of the VFW Hall like his shoes were on fire.

Ellie's eyebrows furrowed. "He isn't staying for dinner?"

I scowled. "I guess not." Seeing him so eager to leave, I cried. If I had any doubts, it was over between us. He just put them to rest.

"Oh, honey." Ellie put her arms around me and then turned to Al. "Give us a minute, okay?"

"You betcha," Al said, looking extremely uncomfortable at this emotional moment.

"Why did Ben leave so soon? Did the two of you have an argument?"

"No. Not really." More tears came at me. "It's just that it's over. Why should he stay?"

"That can't be. I think you have this all wrong. Maybe he doesn't want to leave."

This was silly. She had all this wedding stuff in her head, thinking that happily ever after was out there for everyone. "He can't wait to leave."

Ellie put both hands on the top of her head in amazement. "Oh my God, really? That's what you think?"

"Then why did he get a job in another town? That isn't what a man in love does."

"Men in love do all kinds of things. You don't have the market cornered on that." She took my hand. "I mean, look at Holden Ramsey. He's desperate to marry Magnolia. He'd do anything to marry her."

"That actually sounds right." My boss had become a missile heading to a target with this marriage. So much so that he would lie about the pass he made at me even if it made me look bad.

"In a weird, twisted way."

I picked up my bag. "I'm getting a headache. I think I'll skip dinner, too. You and Al have fun."

"Sure. No problem. I hope you think about what we just discussed. He loves you, Dot."

The general, who had had been talking to Al, had returned to the kitchen area some time ago, and I had lost sight of him. Suddenly, a man in a white T-shirt with an apron tied at the waist was striding across the floor toward us.

"Miss Morgan?" He spoke with a thick Mexican accent.

"Yes?"

"You have a phone call in the kitchen. "

"Really? Who would call me here?"

"It's the police. Officer Oliva." The couple at the next table looked up at the man from the kitchen and then over at me.

"If you'll follow me." He motioned to the other end of the hall. The kitchen of the VFW was much smaller than I had imagined, with two men in white aprons doing most of the work and a busboy dumping dishes into a soapy sink. The man directed me to a wall phone, and when I answered, I found Mary on the other end of the line.

"Thank God I caught you."

Why would Mary be tracking me down at the VFW? "Are the children okay?"

"Yes, they're fine, but your friend Gerald just got arrested."

"Arrested? What for?" Had he and Holden finally had it out about the use of the recording studio?

"Joyce Bishop's murder."

"On what grounds?" It felt like Gerald's father's history was repeating, but in his son's life.

"Joyce's father came in and said he had been given some information that pointed to Gerald."

"What information?"

"I'm not sure, or even who told him this, but our police chief didn't even investigate it. They just hauled Gerald in. I think he could use a friend right now."

"What can I do? I'm not a lawyer."

"No, but you're the nosiest person I know." Mary paused. "I'm not sure if he's going to get a fair shake otherwise."

She was referring to the fact that Gerald was colored and every officer at that station was white. She didn't have to spell it out.

"Gerald's mother has been here trying to get him released, but they won't even talk to her. I told her I'd try to help, so I'm calling you."

"Does he have bail?"

"Not yet."

"Okay, thanks for tracking me down."

When I hung up, I realized the kitchen clatter had stopped behind me. The man who came to get me had kind brown eyes. "Is everything okay?"

"No, not really. The police just arrested someone without investigating the claim against him."

"Yes, we know of this. Was he Mexican?"

"Colored." The surrounding group all nodded, confirming to me they knew all about being arrested without proof. I was discovering there were two worlds in my small town of Camden. I was the lucky one in this room, and I would not forget it.

Chapter Thirty-Two

I felt partly to blame for what was happening to Gerald. I hadn't outright told the police anything. Despite that, I felt guilty. I called the one man who knew every lawyer in town, my father. Dad had worked at the courthouse for most of his life and knew every lawyer who crossed the threshold. As soon as I told him about the situation, he promised to bring in Scotty Bilson to help Gerald navigate his way out of jail.

When I got to the jail, I asked to see Gerald. Officer Jerry looked surprised. It was unusual to see him on the night shift because he normally worked days with Mary. That couldn't be putting him in a good mood, either.

"Why would you want to see Gerald Watson?" Officer Jerry asked with a curl of his lip.

"Because he's my friend and coworker."

He sneered. I never liked this guy. He was the gatekeeper to the rest of the station and made sure that the comings and goings were his design and no one else's. "Your friend, huh? Since when do you have friends like Mr. Watson?"

From behind me came a high-pitched male voice. "You cannot legally deny this young lady entry, so just call back there, and get her clearance. While you're at it, let him know his lawyer is here." Scotty Bilson tipped his hat, revealing a bald pate and a pleasantly rounded face.

Behind him, Ben stepped into the room.

"Me too. I'm with them," Ben quickly stated.

"Keep your wig on. I'll let you see him, for what good you think it'll do. They've caught a murderer, and it's not likely they're going to let him go anytime soon. But why not waste all our time. They've been back there talking to your boss, Mr. Ramsey. Right there shows you justice. They're clearing out the suspects before they charge Mr. Watson."

Why did I feel like their interviewing of Holden was like an exercise in theater to make it look like they had done a thorough investigation. I never would have thought this way before, but now that the unequal treatment had been exposed, I couldn't stop seeing it.

"Again, I ask you, I am Mr. Watson's lawyer and would like access to my client."

Before the officer could continue, a deep voice spoke out from behind us. "No need for that. We've got a lawyer here." When I turned, it was Jasper from the club. His eye caught mine, and he gave a tight-lipped smile.

"So, which is it?" the officer snapped.

"Sorry," I said. "I didn't know if Gerald would have a lawyer yet, so my dad helped me find one."

Jasper nodded. "No need to apologize. Gerald has done a lot for all the guys down at the club, so we were glad to call up Mr. Simmons here."

A man in a dark suit with a tan vest stepped forward. His rounded glasses were perched at the end of his nose. "How do you do?" He extended his hand to me.

"It's nice to meet you. I work with Gerald at the radio station."

"It's nice to meet you, too. Now, let's get down to business and get this young man out of jail."

Jasper stepped closer, this time with another man on his arm. "This is Gerald's daddy, Mr. Watson. He wanted to meet you."

I shook Gerald's father's hand. He was bent over slightly, his back malformed from age. "How are you, sir?"

"Not good. I never thought I'd live to see this happening again. Bishop's the one who accused him, and with Lawyer Simmons's help here, we're going to do everything we can not to let that son of a bitch get away with it again."

"Why would he do that?" I asked.

"Yes," Ben stepped forward, pen in hand. "Did he have some kind of proof?"

"Don't think so," Mr. Watson answered, "but he never needed proof to put a man in jail before."

Whatever happened to justice? Why was there this invisible line that separated the right to a fair trial?

Ben was nodding as he wrote. "May I use what you just said in the *Camden Courier?*"

Mr. Watson pressed his lips together. "I know you mean well, telling our side of the story, son, but printing a story about this might stir up a nest of bees I don't want to deal with."

Of course, he didn't want people to refocus on him. Even though his son was innocent, the chances of the truth being pushed back for someone's narrative were very real.

"I understand," Ben said, putting his pen down. This was the most restraint I'd seen out of Ben in a while. Hadn't I asked him not to print Holden's story? I could only hope he would respect the promise he just made.

"Do you? Really?" Old Mr. Watson said.

Jasper put his arm around Gerald's father. "Maybe you should let the man print your words. No one has ever offered to tell our side of the story."

"And then what happens when Bishop comes after me again?" he asked.

Joe, the leader of The Harmony Kings, stepped forward. "Then we stand behind you. We'll make sure you're safe."

Mr. Watson shifted from one foot to the other. "I don't know about that. People could get hurt."

Officer Jerry, who had been listening with a scowl on his face, tapped his fingers on the counter. "Well, I hate to spoil the party, folks, but there's too many of you to go back there. Choose whichever lawyer you're going to use, and I'll let him, and only him, through. Got me?"

Mr. Simmons stepped forward. "Do you have a list of the charges?"

Officer Jerry shifted. "Actually, he is still being detained."

"Detained, as in there are no actual charges or legal proof that Gerald Watson committed any crime at all?"

"Oh, he did it," Officer Jerry said with the confidence of the ignorant.

"No proof. Let him go. Release him now."

Twenty minutes later, Gerald came out of the back, rubbing at his wrists.

His father grabbed him and embraced his son.

"I got you out."

"Daddy, I didn't do anything. I promise."

"I know you didn't. You're a good boy. Always have been."

Gerald looked over at the assembled crowd. His eyes lit on Jasper and then on Ben and I.

"Thank you. Thank you all," he mumbled as he readjusted his glasses.

As we were about to leave, Leah Ramsey came out with a delicate handkerchief up to her lips. She had been with Holden in the interrogation room and hadn't noticed the collected crowd waiting for Gerald. They entered the lobby area from the back room of the station, and Detective Sprague led her out. "Why is that despicable man not in jail?"

Leah was pointing at our assembled group. The fact that Gerald's lawyer and father stepped up at the word despicable didn't go over well, especially when Wyatt Bishop brought up the rear.

"What the hell? Why is this boy out of jail? Since when do they let guilty men go free?" Wyatt's cheeks were turning a deep red as he glowered at Gerald.

"Guilty until proven innocent, if you please," Gerald's lawyer stated in a cultured accent.

"He did it. This is injustice."

"It's an injustice to put a man in jail based on the color of his skin," Gerald's father said, "but that's what you do best, isn't it?"

"What the hell? Who let you out?" Bishop raised his meaty fists into the air. "What's happening to this country?"

I didn't know what bothered me more, his untrue accusations or his arrogance. I came forward. "What should have happened years ago? Justice is supposed to be blind."

Wyatt Bishop looked seriously confused by my statement. He did not know what I was talking about.

Leah Ramsey shook her head. "Coming from a woman who tried to break up my son's engagement by throwing herself at him. I wouldn't trust a word you say."

I shot a look at Holden, who closed his eyes, trying to shut out his mother and everyone else in the room. His lies were coming home to roost, and I would not let him get away with it. "You need to talk to your son about how he kissed me without my consent. He's been flirting with me since the first day I started working at the station. Bet he forgot to tell you that part, didn't he?"

"Lies, all lies. Just like what Mr. Watson's people are saying. He killed that girl, and we all know it. It was revenge for what Mr. Bishop did to his father. Nothing more. He needs to be put away for life, and no matter what kind of fancy-colored lawyer he gets, I'm sure he will be in prison just like his father was. The apple doesn't fall far from the tree."

Detective Sprague cut in, trying to ease the stress in the room. "Mr. Watson is free to go, and you need to let the police do their job."

"Well, I plan to tell them all about how he used our recording studio without our permission. We'll be pursuing the repayment of fees to us immediately, or we'll have Gerald arrested for that. Mr. Watson, please hand over your keys to the station." Leah's eyes flashed. Gerald pulled a set of keys out of his pocket, and Leah snatched them away and deposited them in her purse. She pulled out the tissue and returned to her show of looking fragile. Holden then took his mother's arm to guide her through the lobby. "Enough. I'm ready to go home, and I don't need you leading me out. I'm not afraid of these men." She pushed her way through the crowd.

As Holden walked by me, he whispered, just out of earshot of his mother, "You're not fired. Meet me at the station in an hour."

Chapter Thirty-Three

I stared at Holden, who leaned against the soundboard, his arms crossed. "Are you sure about this?"

"Not much choice. We've been nothing but static for the last few hours. You've demonstrated that you know how to DJ, and I need a replacement for Gerald immediately. I need you on the night shift from five to eleven for a few days until I can find someone better. Oh, and don't let Uncle George out. We got a complaint from someone in the neighborhood who has a cat in heat. I guess he's been hanging around."

I was excited about the idea of being a real live DJ but had reservations for two reasons. One was his mother hated me and thought I was some kind of seductress, and the other was there no way I was going to spend hours on end talking about the virtues of "Three Coins in the Fountain."

"Can I play what I want to?"

"I don't give a damn what you play. Just keep us on the air."

"I can play the Beatles and Mary Wells?"

"Like I said, play whatever. I never use the top forty line I buy."

"Because your mother won't let you?"

He looked bruised by my comment. "I do what I want. I just have better taste in music."

"Okay, do you really think Gerald killed Joyce?"

Holden, who often put out the impression of a handsome Gregory Peck, looked tired. His shoulders slumped slightly, and I noticed that his hair looked a little thin on the top. "I don't know, but my mother does, and that means he's out at the station."

"I thought you ran this station." It seemed that way when he hired me. Now it was obvious he didn't make a move without his mother. It was also obvious that she controlled the purse strings.

"I do, of course, but it's a family business, and I need to respect my mother's wishes." What he meant was, his mother was paying all the bills, so she got the final decision on everything. Why hadn't I seen this earlier? Charming, debonair Holden was a mama's boy. "Is that why you play all her favorite songs?"

Holden's face changed, and for a moment, that put-together man of the world looked unsure. "They're classics, and our listening audience enjoys them. We are played in most of the medical offices that have speaker systems and radios in town."

"Have you ever stopped to think that maybe they like that music because it's so boring, they can keep their patients calm?"

Holden's eyes turned cold, the blue now tinged with gray. "I really don't care what you think, Dot. If I wasn't desperate to keep the night shift covered, we wouldn't be having this conversation. You've proven you can handle it, so follow the same protocol I do during the day with commercial breaks, and we should be fine." He set his daily schedule next to the microphone and turned one more time to me. "If you have questions, try to work your way through it. I won't be available for phone calls. I need to patch up what's left of my life."

"I didn't think that was a possibility after Magnolia's parents shut you out," I said with a soft smile.

"Probably not." He let out a chest-wrenching sigh. "But I have to try."

After Holden left, I carefully locked the front and back doors to the radio station. No one else would work with me tonight, and after Joyce's murder, I was a little unnerved by it all. The record came to a stop, and I put on the national commercial record while I stacked up my choices for the night. The Beatles, "Chapel of Love" by the Dixie Cups, "A World Without Love" by Peter and Gordon, and finally "I Get Around" by The Beach Boys. Once the commercial ended, I flicked on the microphone. It was hard to realize that people all over Camden were settling down for the evening, with my voice in the background. My own parents didn't even know I'd be on the radio. I had to admit that even though I didn't care for the music choices Holden played, my parents loved it. Sometimes, they stood in front of the stereo and danced around the room.

"Hello Camden. Dot Morgan back at the microphone tonight. I know you expected Jammin' Gerry tonight, but he's, well, he's not able to be here." There was no way I was going to tell the entire world that Gerald had been questioned for murder. I'd had a taste of the unfair treatment he met every day, and the last thing I wanted to do was encourage it. "I'll try my best tonight to play some music you'll love. If you have a request, call me on the KDUD request line. Things have been rockin' and rollin' around the station here, so let's just escape it all with 'Listen, Do You Want to Know A Secret?' Every time I play this one I'm amazed by all the secrets here in Camden. Sometimes I'm afraid to ask."

I put the needle on the record, shut off the microphone, and sat back to take a breath. That hadn't been too hard. Maybe not seeing everyone who was listening was a good thing. I continued this way for the next hour. The request line started ringing, and I was busy trying to spin records and answer the phone at the same time.

One of my calls was Gerald. "Hey there, DJ Dot. Can I stop by?"

"I'm pretty busy."

"I just wanted to talk to you for a minute. I'll even help if I can."

I wasn't sure if it was a good idea. If Leah or Holden found out Gerald was at the station, they would not be happy.

Within twenty minutes, Gerald was tapping at the outer door. There were only a few seconds left on the record, so I ran and opened the door for him, quickly relocking it once he was inside.

"That was fast," I said as I made my way back to the booth.

"There's no traffic in Camden tonight." I let him through the dark lobby area.

"Hold on just a minute."

Gerald took the extra seat in the booth. Uncle George jumped in his lap, deciding he didn't meet his human standards for the moment, and jumped back down. He meowed, and I quickly put him out in the lobby, shutting the door. Once outside, Uncle George's meows took on a more commanding tone. He wasn't too pleased to be in the next room, but I had to do it if I didn't want his voice on the air. I flicked on the microphone. "Well, I guess that last tune was pretty raucous, so here's a lovely soft one for my parents at home." I put on a ballad, shut off the mic, and turned around to face Gerald. "What did you want to talk to me about? How are you doing?"

"I don't know." He shuffled his feet slightly and looked uncomfortable. "I'm scared, Dot. Really scared of what's going to happen next. You know, there was a time when I thought I loved Joyce Bishop? I was only sixteen, and she was such a forbidden fruit. I thought she loved me, too. Then, when I realized I was nothing more than a way to take a jab at her daddy, I broke it off, and she got pretty ugly. Then I hated her." His gaze seemed to melt into me, and I had to look away.

I kept my eye on the needle of the record. Gerald's emotions were raw, and the fact that he was trusting me with this information was a little unnerving. "Did you hate her enough to kill her?"

"That's what the police think, but no. My life went on. That year, I found some new old friends. Fats Domino, Billie Holiday, even The Ink Spots. It was like they were singing directly to me, and that was what helped me to move on with my life. Can you understand that?"

"Yes. I think I do."

The record was near an end, so I readjusted the needle to another song on the album.

"I like your choice of music. I'll bet that fella over at KOOL is spitting nails right now."

"I certainly hope so."

"I, uh, also wanted to say thank you for calling a lawyer and trying to rescue me tonight. That was sweet of you to try."

"And then I found out you didn't need any rescues. Your family and friends had it covered and with a really good lawyer."

"That he is. I wish he had been around for my daddy's case." Gerald stood. "I don't know what lies in the future for the both of us, but I just wanted to say it's been a pleasure getting to know you, Dot Morgan."

I jumped up and hugged him. He was the one true friend I had met at KDUD, and the station would never be the same without him.

After putting on another song, I opened the door to the DJ booth, where Uncle George sprang up from the couch and immediately began meowing and passing through our legs. I walked Gerald to the door, undid the lock, and opened it to let him out.

Gerald reached down and put his hand under my chin and said, "Stay sweet, Gidget."

Finally, I closed the door and locked it.

I returned to the booth and after a few comments, reset the music. It was quiet, just me in the booth. Too quiet. I started stringing together paper clips when I realized Uncle George wasn't bothering me for attention. Where was that annoying cat? What would Leah do to me if I lost her beloved Uncle George? I ran from the booth and unlocked the outside door. I had been so focused on Gerald that I hadn't noticed George making a stealthy giveaway into the dark of night. I called out, "Here, kitty. Uncle George. Here, kitty, kitty." There was a rustle in the bushes, so after propping the door open, I walked in that direction. I figured I only had about a minute before I would need to be back, so I rushed out into the pitch black in the sound's direction. Uncle George sprinted from one bush to the next, the faraway light on the station lighting up the greens of his eyes.

"Come here, Uncle George. The record is almost over. I don't want to have to leave you out here."

He moved, and I lunged, scraping my knee on the soft dirt around the bush. He gave a complaining meow as he struggled to get out of my arms, but I held firm. "I'm not in the mood to hear your owner tell me off because you escaped. I'm sure I'm the one who will get blamed for it." Being familiar with the record, I knew it was in its last ten seconds as the goodbye chords softened over the loudspeaker. I shut the door, dropped the cat, and bolted for the studio. Once inside, I took a quick breath.

"Love it! Now, here's tonight's weather forecast. Excuse the heavy breathing. I was dancing in the booth." It was a lie and a corny one at that, but I'd be crazy to announce I was outside chasing Uncle George. I read off the weather and then put another record on. Once that was finished, I leaned back in Holden's chair, and now that the excitement was over, my body shifted to its real state. Exhaustion. Emotional and physical. I stifled a yawn. I hadn't planned on being the night DJ, and the fatigue was settling in. I closed my eyes, all the while internally warning myself not to fall asleep.

"Hello, Dot."

I immediately recognized the low, slightly clipped accent. It was Morris, Leah's employee.

"Morris? What are you doing here?" I looked at the door. When had he come into the station?

"I'm here on business for my employer." He answered, his hands resting behind his back.

"Please don't let her know about Uncle George. He just got out, but I grabbed him. He's noisy, and he doesn't enjoy being locked out of the booth."

"He's special, just like all the Ramseys. He isn't used to being locked out."

I found it interesting the level of loyalty Morris had for the family he served. Usually, when you get someone away from their boss, a little something about the working conditions slips out, but he was ever-adoring.

"So, that's why you're here?"

Morris looked around the room. "No, I'm afraid not. You've really done well taking over for Mr. Watson here. You're a very smart girl. Tell me, do you have any songs that give you enough time to take a brief break to use the powder room?"

That was a weird question. Did he need me to assist him with something? Did he need help to get Uncle George out to the car? "I haven't been at this job all that long, so I couldn't tell you, although 'Three Coins in the Fountain' is a little on the long side. Trust me, I've heard it enough."

Morris nodded. "Ah, one of madam's favorites. I, too, must admit I enjoy the song stylings of Mr. Frank Sinatra. Why don't you put that one on?"

I looked over at my request list, and unsurprisingly, "Three Coins in the Fountain" was not on it. "Why?"

"Because I'm making a request. That's what you do here, right? Answer requests? That is mine."

Something wasn't right. Morris's cryptic request was strange and a little demanding for such a quiet man. I walked over to the record shelf and pulled out the familiar album. The record I had been playing was about to end, so I unsleeved the album and turned on the microphone.

"Okay, folks. We've had a request for 'Three Coins in the Fountain', and uh," I couldn't ignore the strange anxiety that was shaking through me. "And I would have to say, the three special coins in my life are Mary Oliva, Ben Dalton, and Ellie Monroe. Love you all, and I wish you were all here with me right now. I really do." I set the needle on the record player and prayed at least one of them was listening. I turned off the microphone, and when I turned back to Morris, I saw the same two-pronged weeding trowel he'd been using at Leah's house, but this time, instead of removing a weed, he was aiming it right at me. The tool came down swiftly from his raised hand, and instinctively I veered away. Not fast enough, because the tool bit into my shoulder. I reached behind me and purposely hit the needle on the record, causing it to scratch all the way across the album. A part of me was delighting in the fact there would be no more Frankie with three coins falling into the fountain.

"You shouldn't have done that. Put the record back on." He held the simple gardening tool out in front of me. They still hadn't recognized what killed Joyce, but from the width of the trowel, I would bet this was what he used.

The phone rang, cutting through the air between us. Morris nodded for me to answer it.

"What the hell is going on over there?" Holden was on the other side.

"Uh, well." I didn't know what to say. If I told him Morris was about to kill me, he might just speed the entire process up. I looked at Morris, and if he could read my mind, he shook his head no.

"Put another record on!" he yelled.

"Yes, sir." I hung up and then reached for the microphone. "Sorry about that, folks. Little mishap here at the radio station. I know this might sound unusual, but I'd just like to say I love you, Mom and Dad. Guess I'm getting sentimental in my old age. Now, let's put on a little 'Dead Man's Curve', shall we?" I cued up Jan and Dean and turned back.

"You think I don't know what you're doing, sending a message to your parents? You'll be dead, and they'll never hear it."

"Why are you doing this?"

"For Leah, of course. She's the finest woman in the world, and I can never let bad things happen to her."

"Does that include her son, Holden?"

"Yes. Holden is a troublesome boy, and we constantly have to clean up his messes. We did with Tracy and then Joyce. Tracy was easy. Holden went to the car and one little push. It was over. Joyce, though, was troublesome. Very messy, that one. Bird seed everywhere."

This was interesting because he had stopped using the pronoun "I" and had switched it to "we." "Are you saying that you and Leah have killed these women?"

"Of course not. Leah would never lower herself to such a barbaric action. She's too good for that. No, it's my job to take care of these matters. She does not know all I do for her."

Then I remembered the little brown dots that came out of his pocket when he produced a pill bottle for Leah. It was birdseed. "Let me get this straight. You have taken it upon yourself to kill people for your employer?"

Morris gave a small chuckle, making his rounded cheeks puff out. "She's much more than my employer, young miss."

"Are you romantically involved with Leah?"

He blushed. "Of course not. She deserves better than the likes of me. I'm afraid my love is unrequited, but that doesn't mean that I won't serve her forever."

I had to keep him talking. "You've committed two murders. Aren't you afraid of getting caught?"

This time, he laughed. "Me? Who would suspect the shy little garden man? Everyone underestimates me. They hardly know when I'm in the room. When you have red hair and a dumpy appearance, it's like being invisible. Some people might hate it, but I rather like it."

He was right. He was always somewhere in the background. It was the perfect guise for someone who was out there murdering people.

"You don't need to murder me. I'll just forget you're here, just like everyone else has."

"Don't be silly. You're too smart for your own good, young lady. No, you have to go. It's because of you that Magnolia broke it off with Holden. If you're dead, you can no longer seduce him. Men are the weaker sex, after all. I just must hope that this brings her back into the fold."

"But seriously, these murders center on the Ramsey family. The police are going to narrow down the suspect to either Leah or Holden. They have strong motives for doing this. Had you thought of that?"

Morris looked slightly confused as he pulled his red eyebrows together in a frown. "No one can ever suspect my Leah of any wrongdoing. She's beyond reproach."

"What about Holden, the born loser? How many businesses has his mother supported him with? How many have gone bankrupt?"

He turned his head to the side as if getting a knot out of his neck. "True. He looks like he'd be desperate enough to murder, but I'll fix it. I love her enough to fix anything."

"By killing me?"

"It's a start." He raised the weeding trowel again and started for me. I pushed a chair between us.

"Morris, wait! You should know something." I had to think of something, and quick or I was going to be just like Joyce. I had left as many breadcrumbs as I could think of, but he was right. There was no guarantee anyone listening to the radio knew I was in trouble.

"Leah told me she was thinking of firing you."

Morris's hand stopped in midair, the deadly weapon with its two points poised to make a painful stab into my skin. "You're lying. She wouldn't make a move without me. She depends on me for everything. You're just stalling the inevitable." He rushed me, pointing the trowel at my throat. If he succeeded and hit the carotid artery, I would bleed to death in minutes. This was the last thing Joyce saw before her death.

I reached back and pulled out an album, which crunched in half when he hit it with the tool. I pulled another and threw it at him, hoping to angle it enough that the sharp corners would stop him. It was stupid trying to use an album as a weapon, but it was all I had.

"You don't have to make this so hard. I'm going to win."

"How can you? We're on the air. Half of the town is waiting for their next song and wondering what's going on down here."

"I told you. I'm invisible. No one will suspect me.'

I threw another album at him, but he cut the distance between us and jabbed at me again. I moved away in time, but I was cornered. He plunged the trowel, and I skidded out of the way while Uncle George jumped up on the cabinet, knocking down the glass microphone and hitting Morris on the head. He stumbled backward, then fell onto the floor. He dropped the trowel, and I scrambled to get it before he could pick it back up. Once I did, I held it in front of me, trying to look like I knew how to use it as a weapon, if he should get up off the floor. I reached over to the phone to call the police, but before I could dial the number, there was a pounding on the door. Squinting through the DJ booth glass, I could see the outlines of Ellie and Al through the exterior window of the lobby. I had to cross in front of Morris to get to them and wasn't sure if he might grab me by the ankle and pull me down. He seemed harmless as he held on to his head, a knot rising under his thin red hair.

I made a run for the door, and he grabbed my leg. While reaching for me, he put part of his weight on Uncle George, who then jumped into the fray and scratched Morris's cheek. It was only a simple cat scratch, but enough to give me a second to escape. Uncle George had been on my side, after all.

Fleeing across the lobby, I ran to the door and turned the deadbolt, and Ellie rushed in. "What's going on? You're bleeding." Behind her was Al.

"Thank God, you made it." Morris was now standing at the booth's door. "This young lady called the house and asked me to come down here. She blamed me for all the trouble with Miss Magnolia. She's so desperate for Mr. Ramsey's affections she attacked me after I said I wouldn't further her cause."

"With what?" Al asked as he looked Morris up and down.

He backed up and retrieved the broken glass microphone. "With this. She came after me with it."

"That's not true." I never figured Morris would lie his way out of this. The thing was, his speech was convincing. Morris didn't look like a threatening man. He looked like a victim. "Uncle George did that as well as the scratch on his face."

"Who's Uncle George? I didn't know we had an uncle named George." Ellie asked, her expression mirrored by Al's.

"Uncle George, the station cat."

Al looked around. "That's a great cat."

"He sure is," I agreed.

Ellie touched my cheek. "I think you've lost a lot of blood."

I still had the weeding trowel in my hand, covered in my blood. "He stabbed me with this. Look at the two points. That explains the wound on Joyce's neck."

"I'll be damned," Al said. "We need to get you to the hospital."

Before Al could move, Morris came barreling through the lobby to escape. Al crossed his arms and stood firm in the doorway. "Like I said. Don't go anywhere."

Morris skidded to a stop, then grabbed me around the neck, the piece of glass still in his hand.

"Let me go from here, and our precious little Dot won't get cut." He looked down at me. "Such a sweet little face. It would be a shame if someone were to cut it up with a piece of glass."

"Put the glass down," Ellie said.

"If you touch her with that thing, I'll have you on the floor in a heartbeat. I was my high school's wrestling champ in 1954." Al tried to look fierce, although he'd put on a few pounds since his wrestling days.

"A gamble I'm willing to take." Morris tightened his grip on me. "I'd do anything for her. Even die. I'm her knight in shining armor."

"Who?"

"Leah," I answered. "He's murdered two women for her already. He'll do it. Trust me."

"The police are on their way. I called them after Dot said that crazy stuff on the air. I called before I left the house. Hurting Dot won't solve anything. You're caught, Morris. Put down the glass." I felt a tear coming on as I realized she'd heard me over the radio and done exactly what I wanted.

As Ellie spoke, the red and blue lights of a patrol car pulled up in the parking lot. Morris tightened his grip again, and I was sure he'd go through with it. Suddenly, he let go, raised what was left of the glass microphone, and threw it through the plate-glass window, shattering it into a thousand pieces. He pushed me aside and ran out the broken window, only to be stopped by the patrolmen.

The knight in shining armor had just hit a large red and blue windmill.

Chapter Thirty-Four

I came into the crowded room that held all the women I held dear in my family. That is all except one, the bride. "Where's Ellie?"

Aunt Mavis pounded the floor, going from side to side of the room, straightening things. "She's putting on her wedding dress."

"She has one?" I asked.

"That's what she's reporting. News to me, kid," she replied gruffly. Aunt Mavis had on the most feminine thing I'd ever seen her wear. It was a blue silk dress with a corsage on the shoulder. She wore a blue pillbox hat with a blue lace veil that was artfully designed around a flower. All touches of Ellie's handiwork.

The whole thing about the wedding dress had gone on for so long, I'd stopped asking. Had she thrown something together last minute? She was a brilliant talent with wedding dresses, but it took time. If she had thrown something together, it was a simple sheath.

I heard a throat clear behind me, and I turned to see my cousin standing there.

Ellie was stunning. Her dress was appliqued with lace and tulle, with a sheer panel on the back and classic white buttons going to her waist. The neckline was scalloped and there was a small, manageable train on the back.

"Can you button me up?" Ellie asked. Aunt Mavis marched over and began buttoning the dress up efficiently.

I circled around her in awe. She looked every bit the glowing bride. It was perfect for her. "Where did you get that dress?"

"I made it, of course." She scowled at me for even asking. Where else would she find the perfect dress but in her own sketch pad?

This dress was amazing, and the thing I knew, it had to have taken her weeks to make. I certainly hadn't seen her sewing anything in the last month that looked like this. "When did you have time to make it?"

As Aunt Mavis finished buttoning, Ellie came to me and put her hands in mine. "I made this dress ten years ago. One thing about being the goofy spinster cousin, you have a little time on your hands. Once I made it, I was ready to be a bride, but nobody was offering, so I stuck it in a box in the back of my closet at home and decided to live in the present, not the future."

"Good policy if I've ever heard one. Live in the present," my mother chimed in.

"Yes, and I'm pretty happy with what's going on today." She started to tear up, and I gave Ellie a hug. We held each other until Aunt Mavis pulled us apart.

"Enough of that. You can cry all you want after our girl goes down the aisle. We will report to that chapel ship-shape."

My mother came over with a lace-edged handkerchief and dabbed at my cheek. "It's fine to cry on a day like today. We all love our Ellie." Somehow, at that moment, my mother had said just the right words. We loved Ellie and were so happy for her...happiness. My mother's secret writing was improving, and she had now converted her romance into a mystery and would call me nightly with the latest chapter updates. I loved that about her. She might have been twenty years older than I was, but she was still searching for and discovering things that made her happy. There was a lesson there, especially as I was trying to deal with Ben's move.

When we started the wedding march a few minutes later, Al and Ben waited on the other side of the church. All eyes were on Ellie, but mine were on Ben as he stood there with his hands folded in front of him. He was so handsome in his navy blue suit, and as I stared at him, I realized he was looking back at me. We shared quiet smiles that said more than the last words we uttered. Sometimes, a feeling shared between two people transcends words.

Ellie and Al exchanged vows, and as they did, I felt my world quiver on its axis. It had shifted, and now I was living in my new today. Ellie was married, and with that marriage would come the course of shared lives. I would miss our closeness so much, but knew this was her dream coming true.

After the wedding, we attended the reception in the VFW Hall which had been decorated by Ellie's and my parents with white wedding bells and silver garland. There was still a slight odor from the cigarettes and beer usually prevalent in the venue, but it was exactly right for Ellie and Al.

Ellie had chosen The Harmony Kings to perform live music, and the crowd was on their feet, dancing most of the time. Ellie, her cheeks red from spinning around the floor, came over to the table where I was taking a break. I had danced with Ben some, but we both knew he was due to leave for Dallas right after the reception, and it was like we had already said goodbye. Our conversation was brief, almost formal.

"Are you going to be all right, cousin?" Ellie asked.

I gave her a little smile. "Sure, but I am going to miss having you around all the time to bounce things off of."

"You mean like your latest involvement with the town's crime rate?"

I laughed. "Stop. It's not that bad."

"Let's see. Two new jobs. Two murders. If I didn't know better, I'd say you have a curse."

I pushed at her shoulder. "I do not."

"Yeah, well, leave the dead people part off your resume. Listen, I don't know if I've told you this lately, but I love you, and I'm going to miss you, too."

"You aren't moving away, like other people in this room."

Ellie glanced at Ben, who was dancing with my mother. "Give it time. I don't think you two are finished yet."

I only wished I could believe her. Ben was moving on to the next chapter in his life, and I was here trying to figure out if I had a job or even wanted one. After what happened at the radio station, it came out that Morris was deeply in love with Leah and would do anything for her, including commit murder. While she was continually rescuing Holden, he was making sure whatever was in her path was eliminated. Now, it seemed Holden had had enough of life on the radio. He closed the station and listed it for sale. Without Morris killing anyone in the way of his happiness, I wasn't sure where Holden would end up. Was he strong enough to strike out on his own without having Morris there to clean up after him? Frankly, even after my schoolgirl crush, I didn't care what happened to Holden Ramsey.

"Promise me this. Don't be afraid to try new things. I heard you on the radio, and I have to say, you surprised me. You did a fantastic job, and I heard the radio station was finally something that people under fifty wanted to listen to for a while, at least. You are a talented, smart woman, and you should never sell yourself short."

"I can't be a DJ. I trained to be a secretary."

"Don't be afraid to grow, little cousin. That's all."

Chapter Thirty-Five

Holden asked me to return to the radio station to get my last check and to help him pack up a few things. As much as I wanted to avoid him, I needed that check. Arlene had been kind enough to keep my share of the rent the same until I could find a new roommate, so if I could find a new job, I'd be fine.

It felt funny coming back to the station. The first thing that rocked me was how quiet it was. I was used to the constant radio broadcast in the background. Holden's voice, commercials, "Three Coins in the Fountain." Today, it was quiet and dark with the plate-glass window boarded up, and after my experience with Morris, it made a chill run down my spine. Holden was working in the DJ booth, packing things up. His attitude was all business now. No more flirting or joking around. What did it feel like to realize your mother's manservant killed people for you? He had to blame himself.

I was about to take the neon KDUD sign off the wall when Holden came into the room. "Keep that up. We have an interested buyer coming to look at the station."

"Really? We do? That's great."

"Yeah. Great. I'd keep the place, but without the infusion of cash from Magnolia's family, I'm having to liquidate everything. I'll be living out of my car before all this is over."

"Have you heard anything from Magnolia?" I asked.

His lips thinned. "Nope, and neither has anyone else. It seems after we called off the wedding, she packed up her stuff and headed to some place called Haight-Ashbury in California. Something about being a part of the

Beat Generation? I think she did it just to get away from her mother."

I'd heard a little about people my age gathering in this area of California, but it would probably go by the way of the hula hoop. A temporary notion. There was tapping on the glass behind us. I turned to see Gerald, his father, and a middle-aged woman dressed in yellow, wearing a floppy hat.

Holden opened the door. "Mrs. Morrison, so nice to see you." He nodded at Gerald. "And Gerald, what are you doing here?" Holden straightened his shoulders. Even though Gerald was no longer a suspect in the Joyce Bishop case, Holden didn't look comfortable around him.

Gerald frowned. "What do you think I'm doing here? I am looking at the station with my real estate agent."

Holden's eyebrows shot up. "Your what?"

"He's looking to buy the place." His father explained, a little smile on his whiskered face.

"You? I'm surprised. I didn't think you had that kind of money."

Gerald pushed his way past Holden, ignoring the slight. "Hello, Dot."

"It's so good to see you again." I hugged Gerald and then shook his father's hand. "Mr. Watson, we meet again."

"Nice to see you, young lady."

"Well, let's look around, shall we?" Mrs. Morrison said, her hat flapping against the darkness of the vacant station.

Gerald took hold of my elbow. "If we can buy the station, it's going to be a partnership. Me and Joe are putting our money together. We figure the money we could make with the studio will hold up the expenses of running the station."

"Really? That's great." I said as we walked toward the recording studio half of the building.

"I heard you on the radio, and I have to say you were surprisingly good. If you ever feel you want me to slot you in for a time, I'd be willing."

Wow. Coming from Gerald, that was a tremendous compliment.

"I was just filling in for you, but thanks for the offer."

"You got what it takes, Dot. If we get this place, you're welcome here anytime, although we'll be cutting out the receptionist job until we have actual money to pay someone."

Mrs. Morrison came up behind us. "Well, what do you think?"

"I think I'd like to make an offer," Gerald answered.

"You know you might run into opposition from part of town," Holden said.

"You mean the Wyatt Bishops out there? Let them complain. If I buy it fair and square, there's nothing they can do."

I admired Gerald's bravery, but I also knew that Holden was right. A nonwhite business didn't happen very often in Camden. It was high time for a change.

After Gerald and his father left with his real estate agent, we finished clearing out our belongings, and I said goodbye to Holden.

"Thanks for the job. I wish it had lasted longer."

"I wrote you a letter of recommendation. It isn't much." He handed me a sealed envelope and then took hold of my hand. "Good luck."

"You too."

As I started to go, Holden went back to putting things in boxes. His head bent, he looked older and a little less polished. So much of his life had been catered to suit him. Now he was on his own, and it was like the years he had been coddled were slipping away, returning him to his true age.

That night, I sat in my empty apartment, the want ads in front of me. My hair was up in large round curlers just in case I had to go out for an interview tomorrow. There weren't many jobs in a town our size, and I thought about the possibility of moving to Dallas. I could find a job there quickly, and, well, Ben was already there. We could try again. There were so many emotions at the end that we had trouble speaking to each other. Now, the only emotion I felt was lonely. Left behind. I was the only one left living this life. Ben, Al, and Ellie had all changed.

I put my hand on the phone, trying to get the courage to call Ben. I had his number on a slip of paper propped up against my kitchen wall. What would I sound like when he answered the phone? Desperate? That was hardly appealing. I took my hand off.

What was wrong with me? Ellie said I was a strong, smart woman. Maybe

I needed to sew my wedding dress during my lonely spinster nights. I put my hand back on the phone. Maybe being an independent woman meant you didn't have to wait around for the man to think about calling you. I could call him myself. I picked up the receiver, my eyes focusing on the paper, but then the jarring sound of someone knocking on the door startled me so much I nearly dropped it.

"Dot?" The muffled voice on the other side was instantly recognizable.

"Ben?" I jumped up to the door, realizing my hair was in curlers. I started pulling them out even though my hair was only partially dry. I straightened my nightgown and grabbed a sweater to put over me. What was I doing? This was Ben, yet here I was, acting like a teenage girl.

When I opened the door, a spread of roses was eye to eye with me. "What are you doing here?"

"I don't know. These are for you." He handed me the roses. They were pink and fragrant, if not a little droopy.

Where had he found roses this time of night? "They wilted a little. I got them from a florist in Dallas this afternoon."

"You bought these for me this afternoon?" I know I sounded like a crazy woman parroting what he was saying, but it was all so confusing.

"Yes. I did. I need to ask you something." Ben fell to one knee. I was about to ask him if he was all right when it occurred to me what he was doing.

"Ben?"

"Will you marry me, Dot Morgan? I've been in love with you since the first day I laid eyes on you, and I don't think I can stand living without you."

My head was spinning, and my hearing felt diminished. Ben Dalton wanted me to marry him. Did I want to marry him? What about Dallas?

"I thought you had a big job in Dallas. I told you I wasn't ready to leave Camden."

"You did, and that's why I quit."

"You did not."

"I did. They were going to put me on stories about traffic court. Nolan kept egging me on, but he didn't mention they started crime reporters in fender bender land. Do you know how boring that is? At least if I stayed here, I could work on the real crime stories. Also, it seems to help to be around you. Strange that."

"So, you're back."

"Yes. Will you marry me?"

I didn't know what to say. I had wanted to be a bride, then I didn't. I hadn't even thought about being somebody's wife. They didn't cover that part in the bridal magazines, and I had a suspicion there was a reason for that.

I put my hands on Ben's, and what I said, even I didn't suspect, and I'm pretty good at detecting things.

"Yes."

Acknowledgements

I would like to thank Glenn Chisman, who DJ'd under the stage name Glen Richards, for helping me learn the world of radio stations in the 1960s. Glen started in 1962 at WMAX in Grand Rapids, Michigan and worked on radio as a DJ, program director, sports announcer and even made recruiting tapes for the Army. He worked all over the country from Atlanta to Houston, and all you have to do is hear his voice to know he's a radio guy. Most of my knowledge of the running of a radio station came from WRKP in Cincinnati, so Glen was an extremely valuable historical resource.

I would also like to thank my agent Dawn Dowdle, who sadly passed away during the writing of this book. She once gave me an award at a conference for being the writer who never gives up, and I will try to continue to live up to that esteemed award, but it will never be as easy to keep trying without her love and encouragement.

Finally, I would like to thank Shawn Simmons and Level Best Books for groovin' along with me in my third Swinging Sixties mystery. I appreciate all you do!

About the Author

Teresa Trent is the author of over 15 books. She started writing cozy mysteries with the Pecan Bayou and Piney Woods Mystery Series. She mainly sets her stories in different geographical areas of Texas and The Swinging Sixties historical series is set just north of Dallas, starting in 1962. You might think with so many books set in the Lone Star state, she was born there, but no. She has lived all over the world, thanks to her father's career in the army. After living in Texas for twenty-five years, she's finally put down roots.

Teresa is a hybrid author, self-publishing early in her career, which led her to traditional publishing with Level Best Books and Camel Press. She is the author of several short stories that have appeared in a host of anthologies. Teresa publishes the blog and podcast, Books to the Ceiling at https://teres atrent.blog where she loves to read the book excerpts of other writers and share in the writing community.

Teresa is a member of Sisters in Crime and lives in Houston, Texas, with her husband and son.

SOCIAL MEDIA HANDLES:
  FACEBOOK:https://www.facebook.com/teresatrentmysterywriter
  TWITTER: https://twitter.com/ttrent_cozymys
  BLOG: https://teresatrent.blog/ (Books to the Ceiling)
  WEBSITE: http://teresatrent.com

GOODREADS:https://www.goodreads.com/author/show/5219581.Teresa_Trent
INSTAGRAM:https://www.instagram.com/teresatrent_cozymys/
BOOKBUB: https://www.bookbub.com/profile/teresa-trent

AUTHOR WEBSITE:
https://teresatrent.com

Also by Teresa Trent

The Twist and Shout Murder

If I Had a Hammer